The Winter of Forever

The Winter of Forever

Mayer Smith

CONTENTS

1	The First Snowfall	1
2	The Old Letter	5
3	The Secret Meeting	9
4	The Edge of the Unknown	13
5	Beneath the Surface	17
6	The Cold Heart	21
7	The Mysterious Visitor	27
8	The Forbidden Dance	33
9	The Whispered Warning	39
10	The Hidden Path	45
11	The Silent Promise	51
12	The Ghost's Visit	57
13	The Broken Trust	63
14	The Night of Secrets	69
15	The Unseen Hand	75
16	The Darkening Sky	81
17	The Mark of the Past	87
18	The Forbidden Kiss	91
19	The Betrayal	95

20	The Coming Storm	99
21	The Echoes of History	103
22	The Shattered Promise	107
23	The Winter Garden	111
24	The Heart's Choice	117
25	The Reckoning	121
26	The Broken Heart	125
27	The Unanswered Questions	129
28	The Fading Light	133
29	The Last Snowfall	137
30	The Final Choice	141
31	The Winter of Forever	145

Copyright © 2024 by Mayer Smith

All rights reserved. No part of this book may be reproduced in any manner whatsoever without written permission except in the case of brief quotations embodied in critical articles and reviews.

First Printing, 2024

1

The First Snowfall

The wind howled as it swept down from the mountain peaks, carrying the first snow of the season with it. The flurry of white flakes painted the landscape in a blanket of stillness, transforming the village into a cold, quiet wonderland. Amara stood at the forest's edge, staring into the snow, her breath forming fragile clouds in the frigid air. It had been five years since she had left this place—five years since she had left behind the memories of her childhood, the closeness of her family, and the warmth of her village. Yet, she was, again, standing in the same spot where the world had once felt like a never-ending adventure.

But today, there was a heaviness in the air that she couldn't shake.

The old path leading into the village was obscured by snow, the familiar dirt path now hidden beneath a sparkling sheet of white. The distant huts of the town stood like silent sentinels, their mud walls blending with the mist. The wind carried the faint sound of children's laughter, a reminder of the life that continued here despite the chill. As Amara took a slow step forward, the crunch of her boots on the snow seemed louder than it should have been. She returned to this village to find answers, answers she didn't even know how to ask.

Her father, the patriarch of their family, had died nearly a year ago, and in his passing, something had awakened in Amara—something buried deep in her bloodline. Her grandmother's passing had brought her to a strange revelation that there were pieces of their family history hidden away in the corners of this village, waiting to be uncovered. She had come back to search for them. But the more she tried to find out, the more elusive they became.

The trees around her creaked in the wind as she walked closer to the village, her mind drifting back to a time when things had been simpler—before her mother left for the city before the whispers of old family secrets had begun to reach her ears, before Nnamdi.

She froze as the memory of him hit her like a sudden wave. Nnamdi.

Her childhood friend—her closest companion, the one who had shared her laughter and her dreams. The one she had shared everything with... until he left.

It had been nearly a decade since she had last seen him, yet the thought of him stirred something deep inside her. The last time they had spoken, the bond they once shared had been as strong as ever, but something had happened to him—something dark that had driven him away. She had tried to reach out and write him letters, but all had gone unanswered—until today.

She hadn't planned on seeing him, not like this, not today. But when she'd arrived at her family's house, Nnamdi had been there, standing at the edge of the village, staring out at the same snow-covered landscape that she now stood in. His back had been to her, but there was no mistaking it.

It was Nnamdi.

Her heart had skipped a beat when she saw him, standing there, just as he had all those years ago—unreachable, untouchable, like a ghost frozen in time. She had tried to call out to him, but the words died on her lips. Instead, she had watched as he turned and disappeared into the shadows of the village, leaving her standing there, feeling as if the years between them had not passed at all.

Amara stood in the silence of the falling snow, unsure of what to do next. Should she follow him? Should she go after him and demand an explanation for his disappearance, for the way he had abandoned her without a word? Or should she leave him to his solitude, as he seemed to want?

She glanced over her shoulder, her gaze falling on the familiar cluster of mud-brick huts, now barely visible through the swirling snow. The village had changed little over the years, but something about it felt different today. An unease in the air made the hairs on the back of her neck stand up. The snowflakes, falling in thick, heavy sheets, seemed to cloak everything in an eerie silence, muffling the world outside.

It was then that she heard it.

A faint sound, barely more than a whisper, coming from the forest. A voice or something that sounded like it. She couldn't quite place it. The wind howled louder, drowning out the sound for a moment, but as the gusts calmed, the whisper returned. She turned towards the forest, her heart pounding in her chest. There was no one there, no visible movement, nothing to explain the unsettling noise.

For a moment, she debated turning back, retreating to the house's safety and her family's warmth. But curiosity—an insistent, almost painful need to understand what had drawn her back to this place—kept her rooted to the spot.

She took a deep breath and stepped toward the trees.

The forest had always felt alive with the sounds of the village, the rustling of animals, the chatter of neighbors, and the footsteps of children running through the underbrush. But today, it was dead quiet, save for the whisper. The deeper she ventured into the woods, the stronger the sensation of being watched became. It wasn't the typical feeling of being alone in nature—it was the sensation of being followed, of something watching her from the shadows.

Suddenly, she heard footsteps behind her.

Amara spun around her pulse quickening. But there was no one there: only the falling snow, the twisting trees, and the cold emptiness of the forest.

She exhaled sharply, her breath coming out in a ragged rush. She wasn't sure whether the chill she felt was from the cold air or the creeping sense of dread that seemed to follow her.

Then, in the distance, she saw it.

A figure.

At first, she thought it was Nnamdi, but the silhouette was too extensive, too broad. And when it moved, it wasn't the easy, familiar way she remembered from their childhood. No, this figure moved with a strange, unnatural grace as though gliding through the snow.

Amara's heart skipped a beat. She knew she shouldn't, but her legs carried her toward the figure. She drew closer as if she were walking in a dream.

The figure turned, its eyes meeting hers, and time seemed to stand still for a moment.

Then it vanished, disappearing into the dense trees without a trace.

Amara stood frozen, her chest tight. The world around her suddenly felt impossibly cold. She blinked, uncertain of what she had just seen.

Was it a trick of the light? Or had she indeed seen something—someone—there?

The only sound now was the whisper of the wind, carrying the memory of a voice she couldn't place.

As the first snow continued to fall, a sense of unease settled deep in her bones. Something was wrong, something beyond the snow, beyond Nnamdi. Something in the village, in the very air itself, was watching her.

Amara didn't know what it was but knew she would find out soon enough.

2

The Old Letter

Amara returned to her family's house, the creaking wooden door opening with a reluctant groan as she stepped inside. The warmth of the hearth hit her immediately, and for a moment, the chill from the forest seemed to melt away. The fire crackled in the center of the room, throwing dancing shadows against the mud walls. The scent of burning wood mixed with the faint trace of incense, a reminder of the rituals her mother had once performed here.

Her eyes moved over the room, lingering on the familiar faces of family portraits that lined the walls. The house had aged since she had left, the once-vibrant hues of the woven baskets and the wooden furniture now faded with time. It felt different now—empty, as if the walls themselves were holding their breath, waiting for something.

She glanced over to the worn chest that sat in the corner of the room, its surface scratched and chipped. It was an heirloom, passed down through generations. Her grandmother had often warned her never to open it, to leave its contents untouched, but that had been years ago. She had long since dismissed those warnings as stories meant to frighten children. Still, her heart fluttered with a mix of curiosity and caution as she approached the chest.

The latch was stiff with age, but after a few forceful tugs, it clicked open. Inside, neatly stacked, were old clothes, bundles of faded cloth, and a few worn leather-bound books. Amara sifted through them, her fingers brushing over the brittle pages, until something caught her attention. A small, yellowed envelope, tucked between two of the books. Her pulse quickened as she pulled it free from its hiding place. The envelope was addressed in elegant script, the ink slightly faded but still legible.

To My Beloved Nnamdi.

Amara's breath caught in her throat. Nnamdi. She could feel the weight of the letter in her hands, the significance of its words pressing down on her. She hesitated for a moment, her fingers trembling, before slowly tearing open the envelope. The paper inside was fragile, the edges frayed with age.

The letter inside was long, written in a familiar hand, but it wasn't her grandmother's writing. No, it was a man's. She recognized the handwriting immediately—it belonged to Nnamdi's father, Ugochukwu, the man who had once been a pillar of the community, before he had disappeared under mysterious circumstances.

Amara sat down on the nearest chair, her legs shaking as she unfolded the letter. She read it slowly, each word seeming to echo in her mind as the world around her seemed to fade away.

My Dearest Amara,

I write to you now, knowing full well that this letter may never reach you. But I must try, for the sake of the love I have always held for you, even if it has been forbidden by forces beyond our understanding.

You and I both know that our families are bound by something far older than our understanding. There is a curse on our bloodlines, one that has haunted us for generations. It is a curse that has already claimed my father and my uncle, and it will not rest until it has taken all of us.

I have tried, in vain, to break the chain, to free us from the darkness that looms over our lives. But there is only one way to do so, and that is to sever the connection between us—between you and me. If we are to survive, if you are to survive, we must stay apart. Our love is the key to the curse, and though it pains me beyond measure, I must leave you now. It is the only way to protect us both.

Please, my beloved, do not seek me out. Do not follow the trail that I have left behind. The answer you seek is in the heart of the forest, where the river meets the land. There, you will find what you need. But know this:

what you find may not be the answer you are hoping for. The curse is a thing of shadows, of ancient magic, and it will not let go so easily.

I am sorry. Please forgive me for what I am about to do.

Yours, forever,

Ugochukwu.

Amara's hands shook as she finished reading the letter, the words swirling in her mind like a storm. A curse. A bloodline tied to darkness. Nnamdi's father had known about the curse, had tried to break it, and had left her, leaving nothing but this letter behind. She could feel the weight of the words pressing down on her chest, making it hard to breathe. Her thoughts raced—was this why Nnamdi had vanished? Was this why he had refused to come back, refused to acknowledge her?

But the letter raised more questions than it answered. The forest. The river. Was this what Nnamdi had been trying to warn her about? Had he known all along that the truth lay buried in the very place she had once called home?

She didn't realize how much time had passed before she felt the sharp coldness of the room settle into her bones. She stood up, the letter still clutched tightly in her hand, her mind spinning. There was no denying it any longer—something was wrong in this village. Something was hidden, something dark and ancient, and it was pulling her back into its grasp.

She needed to find Nnamdi. She needed answers. The only way to get them was to follow the path that Ugochukwu had left for her.

Amara tucked the letter into her coat pocket and turned towards the door, her resolve hardening. She knew what she had to do. But the moment she stepped into the cold air outside, the feeling of being watched returned, more pronounced than before. The hairs on the back of her neck prickled, and she felt a familiar chill creep up her spine.

It was then that she heard the whisper again.

A faint murmur, barely audible over the wind, but unmistakably close.

She whipped around, her heart thundering in her chest. Nothing. The village was still, the air thick with snow and silence. Yet, the feeling remained—the sense that something was lurking, just beyond her reach, watching her every move.

Amara forced herself to steady her breathing. It was just her nerves, she told herself. Just the weight of the letter, the weight of the curse, bearing down on her.

But deep down, she knew. The village was hiding something. And no matter how much she wished otherwise, she wasn't leaving until she uncovered the truth.

The only question now was whether she could survive what she might find.

3

The Secret Meeting

Amara's footsteps were muffled by the thick snow, each one leaving a fleeting imprint in the soft blanket of white that covered the ground. The village was eerily quiet, the usual bustle of daily life silenced by the heavy snowfall. The children who would normally be playing outside had retreated into their homes, and the air felt thick, as though it too was waiting for something.

Amara's mind was in turmoil as she walked, the letter still clutched in her pocket. The more she tried to process Ugochukwu's words, the more questions arose. How much of it was true? And why had Nnamdi's father, a man she had once known as kind and full of life, written such a desperate plea? She could feel the weight of the letter, pulling her towards something she wasn't sure she was ready for.

Her eyes kept darting toward the forest—the same forest that had seemed so inviting and full of possibility in her childhood. Now, it felt dark, as though the trees themselves were holding secrets she wasn't meant to uncover. The path to the village river wound through those woods, and that was where Ugochukwu had said she'd find what she needed. The same path she had walked with Nnamdi years ago.

But that was a lifetime ago.

The wind picked up again, swirling snowflakes around her in dizzying patterns. The moment felt suffocating, as though the storm itself was trying to hide something from her.

Amara quickened her pace.

As she reached the edge of the village, she slowed, her heart pounding. There, standing near the old well by the road, was Nnamdi. He was staring into the distance, his back to her, his broad frame outlined against the snow. The way he stood—so still, so detached—was a striking contrast to the boy she had known. Her heart skipped a beat, but she couldn't bring herself to move forward. The years that had passed between them felt like an insurmountable gulf, and yet, here he was.

He was taller than she remembered, his shoulders broader, his face hardened in a way that made him almost unrecognizable. His once joyful eyes now held a distant, sorrowful gaze, as though he had seen too much of the world's darkness.

Amara felt a wave of emotion surge through her—longing, confusion, and an undeniable pull towards him. But the letter in her pocket reminded her of the danger that lingered in their past. Could she trust him now?

She took a step forward, and the sound of her boots crunching on the snow broke the stillness. Nnamdi's head snapped around, his expression hardening as his eyes locked onto hers.

For a moment, neither of them moved, as if the years between them had frozen the very air.

"Amara," Nnamdi said, his voice rough but steady, as though it had been years since he had spoken her name.

Her breath caught in her throat. It was as if nothing had changed. The way he said her name, the way his gaze lingered on her—there was still something there. But it was buried beneath a layer of pain and secrets, a thick veil she wasn't sure how to peel back.

"Nnamdi," she managed to say, her voice a whisper, barely audible over the wind.

He took a step closer, his dark eyes searching her face, as though trying to read her.

"You shouldn't have come back," he said, his voice low, filled with an edge of desperation. "It's not safe for you here. There's nothing left for you in this place."

Amara's heart clenched. She could hear the emotion in his voice, but there was something more—something hidden beneath his words.

"I found your father's letter," she said, her voice shaking with the weight of the words. "I know about the curse."

For a moment, Nnamdi said nothing. His eyes flickered with something—regret, guilt? Then he looked away, his jaw tightening as he turned his back to her again.

"I told him to leave you out of this," Nnamdi muttered, almost to himself. "I didn't want you to be part of it. I didn't want you to carry this burden. But it's too late now."

Amara's mind raced. The letter. The curse. What had her grandmother and Nnamdi's father been involved in? What had they kept from her? The questions were endless, but the fear in Nnamdi's voice, the sorrow, it was enough to make her want to believe him—enough to make her want to push past all the fear and confusion that had clouded her judgment.

"Nnamdi, you can't just push me away," she said, stepping closer to him. "I need to know the truth. If there's a curse, then it's tied to both of us. We're connected, aren't we? The letter—your father warned me."

His shoulders tensed, and he whirled around to face her, his expression darkening. "I warned you," he snapped. "You shouldn't have come back. You don't know what you're getting into. You don't understand what's at stake."

Amara flinched at his words, but the anger that rose in her chest gave her the strength to keep going. "I don't care what's at stake," she said, her voice rising. "I care about you. And I'm not leaving until I understand everything—until I know why you've been running away from me for all these years."

For a long moment, Nnamdi stood silently, his fists clenched at his sides. The wind howled between them, but neither of them moved.

Finally, he spoke, his voice softer this time. "You think I've been running from you? No, Amara. I've been running from something much darker. Something you won't be able to escape once you know the truth. If you keep pushing, you'll drag us both into a storm you won't survive."

Amara's chest tightened. The look in his eyes, the pain that radiated from him, was more than she could bear. But she stood her ground, her heart pounding in her ears.

"I'm not afraid of the storm," she said, her voice steady. "I want to face it with you."

Nnamdi's gaze softened for the briefest moment, and for a flicker of time, she saw the boy she had once known—the boy who had promised to protect her. But just as quickly, that softness vanished, replaced by the cold, hard mask of a man who had seen too much.

"Then meet me tonight, at the edge of the forest," he said, his voice low and urgent. "I'll show you what you need to see. But you need to understand, once you cross that line, there's no going back."

Amara nodded, her heart pounding. "I'll be there."

Without another word, Nnamdi turned and disappeared into the swirling snow, his figure swallowed up by the blizzard.

Amara stood there, her body frozen in place, the weight of his words pressing down on her like a stone. Tonight. The truth was waiting for her. But what truth? And what would she find when she finally stepped into the heart of the darkness he had been hiding from her?

The wind howled again, and Amara felt it deep in her bones—this was no ordinary storm. This was the beginning of something that would change everything.

4

The Edge of the Unknown

The night was colder than Amara had ever felt, the wind biting through the layers of her coat, sending shivers up her spine. The full moon hung low in the sky, casting a pale, ghostly light across the snow-covered village. The usual stillness of the night was amplified by the oppressive silence that seemed to stretch for miles. Even the usual sounds of nocturnal creatures—crickets, the rustle of leaves—were absent. Tonight, the world felt like it was holding its breath.

Amara's boots crunched against the snow as she made her way towards the edge of the forest, her heart beating louder with each step. She could feel the weight of the promise she had made to Nnamdi. Meet him at the edge of the forest, where the trees met the river, and he would show her the truth. But what was the truth? What had he been running from for all these years?

As she walked deeper into the night, her thoughts turned to Nnamdi. The tension in his voice, the fear in his eyes—it had all been so real. She had never seen him like that before. He was always the brave one, the one who never backed down from anything. And yet, tonight, he had been nothing like the boy she once knew. There had been something raw in him, something that made her wonder what had happened to him. What had he seen? What had he done?

Her breath fogged in front of her, and she pulled her scarf tighter around her neck. The path to the forest was familiar, but tonight it felt foreign. The trees, once welcoming and full of life, now loomed over her like sentinels. Their branches creaked in the wind, as though whispering secrets she wasn't meant to hear. Amara couldn't shake the feeling that she wasn't alone, that something was watching her from the shadows.

She reached the clearing where the trees began to thin, the moonlight casting long, eerie shadows across the snow. The river was just ahead, its dark waters flowing with a quiet intensity. The edge of the forest was where she and Nnamdi used to sit, listening to the whispers of the wind, talking about their hopes and dreams. But tonight, it felt different. Tonight, it felt like the end of something—something that had begun long before either of them had been born.

And then, she saw him.

Nnamdi stood at the edge of the river, his back to her, his silhouette stark against the dark water. He was waiting, just as he had said he would be. But something in the way he stood—so still, so unmoving—sent a chill through Amara. He didn't turn when he heard her approach, didn't even acknowledge her presence.

"Nnamdi?" she called, her voice barely above a whisper, swallowed by the wind.

He didn't respond. Instead, he slowly turned his head, his eyes dark and unreadable. "You came."

"I said I would," Amara replied, trying to keep her voice steady despite the unease creeping up her spine. She took a few cautious steps toward him. "What is this place? What are we doing here?"

Nnamdi didn't answer immediately. He just stood there, staring out at the river, his expression distant. For a long moment, Amara thought he might not say anything at all. But then, in a voice that seemed to come from somewhere far away, he spoke.

"The river has always been here, Amara. It's older than this village, older than us. It's a gateway, a place where the past and present meet. It's where the curse began. And it's where it will end."

Amara felt her pulse quicken. The river. The curse. The words sounded strange, like something out of a story, but the intensity in Nnamdi's voice made it all too real.

"What are you talking about?" she asked, stepping closer. "What curse? What do you mean by all of this?"

Nnamdi slowly turned to face her. His eyes were shadowed, filled with a mixture of fear and resignation. "You don't understand. This place, this river—it's bound to us. To our blood. To our families. It's why my father left. It's why I left. We've all tried to escape it, but you can't run from something like this. It follows you, no matter where you go."

Amara felt a knot tighten in her stomach. The air around her seemed to grow colder, and the silence of the forest deepened, pressing in on her from all sides.

"I don't know if I can explain it all," Nnamdi continued, his voice low, as if he were speaking to himself more than to her. "But I'll try. There's something in our bloodline, something ancient. My father knew about it. Your grandmother knew about it. They thought they could contain it, keep it buried, but it's never gone away. It's always been waiting for the right time to come back."

He paused, his gaze flickering nervously to the river, as if afraid to look too long.

"Amara, the curse—it's tied to us. The moment we were born, it set its mark on our souls. We didn't ask for it, but it doesn't care. The moment we were born, we were bound to the river, to the forest, to the darkness that lies beneath it all."

Amara's breath caught in her throat as a cold gust of wind swept through the clearing, rustling the bare branches above them. She could feel the hairs on the back of her neck standing on end, her heart pounding with a mixture of dread and curiosity.

"What happens now?" she whispered, barely able to get the words out.

Nnamdi didn't answer immediately. Instead, he took a few steps towards the river, his face drawn in pain, as if every step was weighing him down.

"There's a place beneath the water," he said quietly. "A place where everything began. If we want to stop it, if we want to end the curse once and for all, we have to go there. Together."

Amara's chest tightened. "What's beneath the water?"

Nnamdi's expression darkened, his jaw clenched. "I don't know exactly. But I know it's where the power comes from. Where the darkness sleeps. It's been waiting for us to come back."

Amara stood frozen for a moment, her mind racing. She had come here seeking answers, but now, standing at the edge of the river, the weight of Nnamdi's words pressed down on her like a lead blanket. The curse. The river. The place beneath the water.

She didn't know if she was ready for whatever was coming, but deep down, she knew there was no turning back.

"Am I supposed to go in there?" she asked, her voice barely above a whisper.

Nnamdi looked at her, his eyes filled with a mixture of sorrow and urgency. "We have no choice. The river won't let us go until we do."

Amara felt a surge of fear, but it was quickly replaced by something stronger—determination. She had come this far. She had to know the truth, no matter what it cost her.

Without another word, she stepped toward the water, her heart pounding in her chest. The river's surface was calm, its dark waters reflecting the pale light of the moon. But beneath it, there was something else—something waiting.

And Amara was about to find out what.

5

Beneath the Surface

Amara could hear the faint rush of the river's current, but the sound was drowned out by the pounding of her own heart. The coldness of the water seemed to seep into the very air around her, and the closer she stepped to the edge, the more the chill gnawed at her skin. The moonlight reflected off the water, casting an eerie silver glow that seemed to twist and writhe, like something alive beneath the surface.

Nnamdi stood beside her, his presence tense and taut, like a coiled spring. His eyes were fixed on the water, but his face was blank, betraying nothing of the turmoil he must have been feeling. She could feel the weight of his silence, the burden of everything unsaid between them.

The air between them was thick with unspoken words—words of warning, of regret, of things left unsaid. But the only thing that mattered now was the river, the darkness waiting just beneath the surface.

"Are you ready?" Nnamdi asked, his voice rough, as though speaking was an effort. His eyes flickered to hers, but there was no comfort in them. Just the same haunted look she had seen earlier. "Once we step into the water, there's no going back."

Amara swallowed hard. The words hung in the air, the gravity of them settling on her shoulders like a heavy cloak. No going back. That's what he had said. And yet, there was no choice. She had already come too far.

"I'm ready," she said, her voice steadier than she felt.

For a long moment, Nnamdi said nothing. His eyes lingered on hers, searching, as if weighing her resolve, but then, without another word, he stepped toward the water. The snow crunched under his boots, his movements deliberate. He waded into the river, the icy water rising quickly around his boots.

Amara hesitated, her feet glued to the earth, as though the ground itself was trying to keep her from moving forward. She could feel the pull of the river, as though it was calling to her, drawing her in. Her thoughts raced. Was she truly ready for what lay ahead? What would they find beneath the surface? The curse? The darkness?

With a deep breath, she forced herself to move. Her boots sank into the wet earth, and with every step, the cold grew more unbearable. The water crept higher, up to her ankles, then her knees. Each inch she moved forward was a struggle. Her heart was in her throat, and her mind was spinning with doubts, with questions. But she had no choice. She was already too deep, too far into this mystery to turn back now.

Finally, she was standing beside Nnamdi, the cold water now at her waist. The current was stronger than she had expected, pulling at her legs, tugging at her with a force that seemed almost unnatural. She could feel the weight of the water, the pressure building around her, as though the river itself was alive and breathing.

"Keep your eyes on me," Nnamdi said, his voice barely audible over the sound of the rushing water. "Whatever you do, don't look away. Don't get distracted."

Amara nodded, though the words did little to reassure her. Her gaze remained fixed on Nnamdi as he waded deeper into the water, the darkness of the river growing thicker around them. The cold was unbearable now, and the current pulled at her legs, threatening to drag her under. But she couldn't stop. She had to keep going. She had to follow him.

The water rose higher, swallowing her waist, her chest. She could feel the tendrils of the river's chill seeping through her clothing, sinking into her skin, freezing her to the bone. The moonlight grew fainter as the darkness of the river consumed everything around her. She couldn't see where the water ended, only the cold, empty blackness that stretched endlessly before her.

Then, just as the water reached her shoulders, something happened.

The river, which had been flowing steadily, suddenly stopped. The current that had been pulling at her legs vanished in an instant. The stillness was suffocating. The air felt heavier, thicker, as though the very atmosphere had changed. She stopped moving, her breath catching in her throat.

Nnamdi was beside her, his hand gripping her arm tightly. His eyes were wide, scanning the water, and his lips were pressed into a thin line.

"Stay close," he whispered, his voice strained, as though he was fighting to keep his composure.

Amara barely had time to react before the water beneath her feet began to ripple. It wasn't the current—it was something else. Something… alive. The water seemed to churn, twisting and writhing, as if the river itself had a pulse.

A shadow passed beneath them.

Amara gasped, her heart racing as she instinctively took a step back. The water had turned darker, the moonlight now completely obscured by an unnatural fog that hung over the river. The surface rippled again, this time with more force, as though something large was moving beneath them.

"Nnamdi!" she cried, her voice panicked, but he held her firm.

"Don't look down," he warned, his voice sharp. "Whatever you do, don't look down."

But it was too late. The curiosity that had been building inside of her was too much to resist. Her gaze slipped toward the water, and that was when she saw it.

A shape—a dark, shifting mass—was rising from the depths. It was enormous, its form vaguely humanoid but twisted and distorted, its limbs long and sinewy, covered in scales that glistened even in the darkness. Its face was obscured by the swirling water, but Amara could feel its eyes on her, the cold weight of its gaze piercing through the water and straight into her soul.

Her breath caught in her throat. It was like nothing she had ever seen before—part man, part beast, part something else entirely.

"What is it?" she whispered, her voice trembling.

Nnamdi didn't answer. He only tightened his grip on her arm and pulled her back. "It's the guardian," he said, his voice tight with fear. "It's the thing that watches over the curse. It's been waiting for us."

The creature's form was slowly emerging from the depths, its long, clawed fingers reaching toward them. Its body shimmered with an eerie, otherworldly glow, and the air around them seemed to grow colder with each passing second. The temperature had dropped so much that Amara could see her breath in front of her, swirling in the frozen air.

Nnamdi's voice was a strained whisper now, as if the creature's presence was suffocating him. "We need to reach the heart of the river. The stone beneath the water. It's the only way to end this."

Amara didn't have time to question him. All she could do was focus on the river, on the darkness, on the creature that was slowly rising from the water. Her pulse was a drumbeat in her ears, drowning out everything else.

And then, with a sudden, violent movement, the creature lunged.

The river surged, and Amara's feet were swept out from under her. The cold water rushed up around her, pulling her down, pulling her into the depths of the river.

She gasped, her lungs filling with water, but Nnamdi's hand was still gripping hers.

He was pulling her down with him, down into the darkness, into the heart of the river.

And Amara knew, in that instant, that whatever lay beneath the surface, it was something far more terrifying than she had ever imagined.

6

The Cold Heart

Amara's lungs burned as the cold water rushed around her, swirling and suffocating. Her vision was blurry, the darkness beneath the surface consuming her like a living entity. She tried to scream, but the water filled her mouth, choking the sound. Her limbs flailed in the blackness, desperate to find something solid, but the river offered no mercy. Every instinct in her body screamed to break free, to swim to the surface, but the weight of the water pressed her down, its force growing stronger with every passing second.

And then, just as her vision started to fade, a hand gripped hers.

It was Nnamdi's hand. Strong, steady, pulling her through the torrent. His touch, though cold and clammy, was the lifeline she needed. She gasped, forcing her lungs to fill with precious air as he yanked her toward him.

"Don't let go!" he shouted, his voice a strangled sound in the depths.

Amara's head spun with panic, but she nodded, clutching his arm as he dragged her through the water. She couldn't see much; everything around them was a blur of movement and shadow. There was something else beneath the surface—a presence, as though the very water was alive, reaching for them, pulling them deeper into its grasp.

The cold was unbearable, seeping into her bones, numbing her thoughts. She could feel herself growing weaker, her body no longer responding as it should.

"Hold on!" Nnamdi's voice came again, a strained whisper this time, as though it were coming from miles away. He pulled her harder, and

Amara felt the pressure of the river's current slacken. The further they went, the more she realized the water wasn't pulling at them anymore—it was pushing them.

They were nearing something. Something in the depths.

Her eyes fought to adjust to the darkness, but all she could see was the shifting outline of Nnamdi, his face grim and determined. For a moment, she thought she saw something else—an unnatural glimmer beneath them, like a glint of polished stone, an object that had been waiting for centuries.

And then she saw it.

A jagged, black rock rose from the riverbed, its surface slick with algae and decay. It jutted out of the water, as if it were a monument or a throne, ancient and unyielding. The stone pulsed with a strange, cold energy, sending a chill up her spine.

The river had led them here.

Nnamdi reached for the stone, his fingers brushing against its rough surface. "We're almost there," he whispered, though his voice was strained with exhaustion. "Just a little more."

Amara tried to push herself forward, her body aching with the effort, but it was like moving through treacle. Every inch was a struggle. Her legs felt heavy, her arms weak. The cold had seeped so deep into her that it was hard to tell where the water ended and her body began.

Nnamdi's grip tightened on her arm, pulling her closer to the stone. The moment they reached it, he gripped the ledge and hauled them both up, dragging Amara from the water. She stumbled, her feet slipping against the slick rock, but she managed to steady herself.

They were on the stone now, standing in the heart of the river, as though the water itself had parted to reveal this ancient structure beneath. The stone was cold—colder than anything Amara had ever felt before. It hummed with a strange power, a vibration that rattled through her bones.

She tried to catch her breath, but the air felt heavy, thick with something she couldn't place. The world around them was still, deathly quiet. The sound of the river had muted, as though they had crossed some threshold where even the water dared not disturb them.

Nnamdi collapsed beside her, gasping for air. His clothes clung to him, soaked and heavy, but his eyes were fixed on the stone, his gaze locked in a mixture of fear and reverence.

"We're here," he said softly. "The heart."

Amara looked down at the stone beneath them. There was something etched into it—grooves and patterns that seemed familiar, like something she had seen before, in old stories, in her grandmother's warnings. The symbols were ancient, carved with precision that suggested a language lost to time.

A cold shiver ran down her spine as she realized they weren't just standing on a stone. The stone was alive. She could feel it. It pulsed beneath her feet, a slow, steady rhythm, like a heartbeat.

But there was something wrong with it.

"Do you hear that?" Amara asked, her voice barely a whisper.

Nnamdi didn't answer immediately. He closed his eyes, as if listening, too. The silence around them grew thicker, more oppressive.

And then, she heard it. A low, grinding sound, coming from deep within the stone, as though something ancient was awakening.

The stone trembled beneath them. Amara felt it before she heard it—the vibrations running through the surface, rattling her teeth. A growl, deep and guttural, echoed through the water, reverberating in her chest.

Nnamdi's eyes widened in horror. "It's waking up," he muttered, more to himself than to her. "It's been waiting."

A dark shadow rippled across the water, swirling around them like a living thing. The air grew colder still, and Amara could see her breath fogging in front of her, though it was clear the temperature had dropped far below freezing. The pulse from the stone quickened, matching the beat of her heart.

Suddenly, the water around them surged. The river seemed to come alive, swirling violently, its dark surface twisting into unnatural shapes. The shadow beneath the water grew larger, more distinct.

Amara's blood ran cold. She saw it.

A shape was rising from the depths, a silhouette emerging from the river as if the water itself had birthed it. The creature was huge, monstrous, its body covered in dark, glistening scales. Its eyes were hollow, black pits of nothingness, but they fixed on her and Nnamdi, burning with a cold intensity.

It was the guardian. The one Nnamdi had spoken of. But now it wasn't just a creature of the river. It was something more—a manifestation of the curse, something bound to the very stone beneath their feet.

The ground beneath them shook, the stone vibrating with increasing force as the guardian's massive form emerged from the river, its limbs long and sinewy, its claws scraping against the rock.

Nnamdi grabbed her arm, his grip tight with fear. "We need to stop it," he said, his voice barely a whisper. "We need to break the seal."

Amara's heart raced, her thoughts scattered. The seal. The curse. What was it? What had her grandmother known? What had Nnamdi's father hidden from them?

The guardian's mouth opened, revealing rows of sharp, jagged teeth. Its growl reverberated in Amara's chest, a sound of hunger and wrath.

Nnamdi turned to her, his eyes desperate. "The stone—it's the key. The curse is tied to it. The only way to end this... we have to break the heart."

Amara didn't understand. She didn't know what to do, but she knew one thing: they had to act fast, or they wouldn't survive whatever it was that had been awakened in the heart of the river.

With trembling hands, she reached toward the stone. It was cold, colder than she had imagined, but as her fingers brushed against its surface, a pulse of energy shot through her. The stone throbbed, its vibration growing stronger, louder, and the river around them seemed to shudder in response.

In that moment, Amara knew that the battle for her soul—and for Nnamdi's—was only just beginning.

7

The Mysterious Visitor

The stone thrummed beneath Amara's fingertips, its cold surface radiating an ancient, unsettling energy. Her hand shook as it lingered there, the vibrations pulsing through her like a heartbeat of something alive, something that had slumbered for eons. The guardian, that monstrous shape in the water, was still there, its massive form rising from the depths, its eyes fixed on her with an unyielding gaze. But the pulse from the stone was growing louder, louder still. It was as though the stone itself was alive, and it had begun to recognize her touch.

For a moment, everything around her seemed to still. The air became thick, pressing in on her chest, suffocating. The water was eerily calm, the surface barely moving as the creature hovered just beneath the ripples. But it wasn't just the river that was still—it was as if the entire world had frozen in time.

Nnamdi stood beside her, his breath coming in shallow gasps. His hand clutched hers, his grip firm, but his eyes were wide with panic, his gaze darting between her and the creature. The tension between them was palpable, the uncertainty, the fear. They were standing on the precipice of something they didn't fully understand, and the more they lingered, the more they could feel the ground shifting beneath them.

Suddenly, without warning, the surface of the stone cracked. A sharp, echoing sound rang out, slicing through the tense silence, and Amara recoiled as the fissures spread like veins, creeping outward across the surface. The pulse she had felt moments before now exploded in a violent rush, a wave of energy that knocked her back, sending her stumbling into the water.

The guardian stirred in the depths, its massive eyes narrowing as the stone cracked even further. Amara's heart thudded painfully in her chest as the cold water surged around her. She scrambled to her feet, her hands trembling as she tried to regain her footing, but it was too late. The stone was breaking apart, and the river was beginning to move again, churning with growing violence.

"Amara!" Nnamdi shouted, his voice strained, but she couldn't hear him over the roar of the water, over the sudden cacophony that seemed to rise from the very heart of the river. The guardian let out a terrifying, guttural growl as the stone split wide open, the black cracks now glowing with an otherworldly light.

For a split second, Amara thought she saw something in the glowing cracks—something shifting in the shadows beneath the stone. Her breath hitched in her throat, and she instinctively reached out toward the stone, but before her fingers could touch the surface again, the ground beneath her feet seemed to dissolve.

A violent wave shot up, knocking her off balance and sending her tumbling backward into the water. Her vision spun, the cold river swallowing her whole. As she struggled to keep her head above the surface, she could feel something pulling at her, something in the depths of the river, something darker than the water itself.

But then, just as she thought she would be dragged under, something sharp and firm grabbed her arm and yanked her upward. Gasping for air, she looked up, her mind still reeling from the sudden chaos. And there, standing beside her, was a figure.

The mysterious visitor.

Amara's heart stuttered in her chest. The figure was cloaked in shadows, their face hidden by a deep, hooded cloak. The air around them shimmered with a strange energy, like a cold mist clinging to their skin. For a moment, Amara thought she might be seeing things—perhaps the cold and the water had numbed her senses, playing tricks on her. But no, the figure was real. It was standing right there, looking down at her with an unreadable expression.

Nnamdi had fallen back in shock, his eyes wide with disbelief. He knew this person.

The figure extended a hand, their movements graceful but deliberate. "Amara," a low, melodic voice said, soft but commanding, echoing through the air like a whisper carried on the wind. "I've been waiting for you."

Amara's breath caught in her throat. "W-who are you?" she gasped, her voice hoarse from the cold.

The figure didn't immediately respond. Instead, they glanced toward the river, their hooded gaze sweeping over the churning waters. The guardian, now fully revealed, was lurking just below the surface, its immense form swirling with an angry, unnatural power. But the figure didn't seem intimidated.

"What is this?" Amara asked, her voice trembling. She could barely process what she was seeing—this strange, mysterious person who had appeared out of nowhere, the guardian in the depths, and the stone that had cracked open with such force. Everything felt like it was spiraling out of control, and she was helpless to stop it.

The figure turned back toward her, their eyes gleaming with an otherworldly light beneath the shadows of the hood. "I am neither friend nor foe," they said, their tone cryptic. "But I have come to offer you a choice."

Nnamdi took a step forward, his voice shaking with disbelief. "You—how did you find us?"

The figure's gaze never wavered from Amara, their voice growing softer. "I knew the moment you arrived. I knew you would come to the river."

Amara's mind was spinning. She had so many questions—too many to ask at once. But one thing stood out, a thread that pulled at her mind with increasing urgency. "You knew I would come?" she repeated, her voice barely a whisper. "But how? What is this place? What is the heart of the river?"

The figure's expression remained unreadable. "The river is older than this village. It is the birthplace of all things—both life and death. It flows with the blood of your ancestors, and it holds the secret to your fate."

The words landed like a heavy blow. The river... her ancestors... her fate? Amara's stomach turned, a deep sense of dread rising within her. This wasn't just a river. It was something far darker, something that tied her family to its depths in ways she couldn't yet understand.

The figure's hand reached out, palm up, toward the broken stone. "You must decide," they said. "What do you seek? Power? Freedom? Revenge?" They paused for a moment, their eyes locking onto Amara's with an intensity that made her blood run cold. "Or do you seek the end?"

Amara swallowed hard. She could feel Nnamdi's presence beside her, his unease palpable. His face was drawn, his expression conflicted. He didn't trust this stranger, and neither did Amara, but something about the figure's presence called to her, tugging at the deepest parts of her soul.

"I... I don't understand," she murmured. "What do you mean, the end?"

The figure's lips curled into a faint smile, but it didn't reach their eyes. "The curse that binds this place, that binds your family, can only be broken by those who have the power to face it. And that power," they said, "lies within the heart of the river."

The guardian let out a low growl from the water, and Amara glanced at the creature, its massive form now fully visible, its eyes glowing with an unsettling intelligence.

Amara turned back to the figure. "What do I have to do?" she asked, her voice shaking. "Tell me what I need to do."

The figure's smile deepened. "That, my dear, is for you to decide. But know this—once you make your choice, there will be no turning back."

The air around them seemed to pulse with the weight of that decision. Amara could feel the pull of the river, the gravity of everything that was happening, pushing her toward something she wasn't sure she was ready to face.

The guardian's growl grew louder, the ground beneath them trembling, and the shadow of the mysterious visitor seemed to grow darker, more insistent.

Amara closed her eyes, drawing a deep breath. It was time. There was no escaping it anymore.

The choice was hers.

8

The Forbidden Dance

The air around them had thickened, as if the very atmosphere had grown heavier with each passing second. The river's low hum seemed to vibrate through the ground beneath Amara's feet, its dark waters still and unyielding, holding secrets that had festered for centuries. The mysterious figure, cloaked in shadows, stood motionless before them, the weight of their presence pressing down on Amara like a physical force. She felt the pull of something ancient, something primal, awakening in the depths.

The guardian remained in the water, its form partially submerged, but its massive eyes never left Amara. They glowed with an unnatural light, burning like embers, and Amara felt their gaze pierce through her, as if the creature was reading her very soul.

"You're not afraid," the figure said, their voice soft but carrying an unmistakable edge of authority. "That's good. It will serve you well in the dance."

"The dance?" Amara repeated, her voice trembling despite herself. The words hung in the air, mysterious, ominous. Her thoughts raced, scrambling to understand, to make sense of what was happening, but nothing about this moment felt right. Nothing about this place felt real.

The figure's hood shifted, and though their face remained hidden, Amara felt their gaze sharp upon her, as if they could see every doubt, every fear swirling within her.

"The forbidden dance," the figure repeated, their voice colder now, almost mocking. "It is the only way to break the bond between you and the river. The only way to set yourself free."

The river's current swirled around them, the dark water whispering as if alive, and Amara could feel a strange heat rising in her chest. The stone beneath her feet pulsed, its cold vibrations still thrumming through her body. But there was something else now—an unspoken challenge hanging in the air, daring her to act. To give in.

"Tell me," Amara whispered, her voice barely audible over the rushing water. "What do I have to do?"

The figure didn't immediately respond. Instead, they moved—swiftly, fluidly, like a shadow in the night, their cloak swirling around them as they approached the edge of the stone. Their hand reached down toward the water, fingers brushing lightly across the surface.

"Dance," they said, their voice growing distant, almost ethereal. "The river calls for it. And you must answer."

The words resonated deep within her, as if the river itself had whispered them into her soul. Amara felt the cold sweat begin to bead on her forehead, her heart racing. The tension in the air had become unbearable, and the weight of the river's presence was now a physical force, crushing her. The guardian stirred, its enormous body shifting in the depths, and the river began to churn once more.

For the briefest of moments, Amara hesitated. How could she—how could any of them—dance with the river, with the cursed waters that had taken so much? But as she looked down at the stone, at the glowing cracks that ran through its surface, she felt something stir within her. A need. A call. A longing that she couldn't explain.

The figure stepped back, watching her with a keen, expectant gaze, their eyes gleaming beneath the hood. "It has already begun," they said. "The river knows you, Amara. It waits for you to remember."

A strange sensation fluttered in her chest, and before she knew it, her body had moved of its own accord. Her feet slid against the slick surface of the stone, her arms raising as if guided by an invisible force. The air around her began to hum, vibrating with an energy that sent shivers down her spine.

Nnamdi's voice broke through the silence, urgent and pleading. "Amara! No! Don't listen to them!"

But it was too late. The first step had been taken.

Amara didn't know why, but she began to move. Her feet shifted, first tentatively, then with more purpose, like the river's pulse had reached inside her, guiding her every motion. The ground beneath her feet seemed to disappear, and for a moment, she was no longer standing on stone. She was weightless, suspended between the earth and the sky.

The rhythm of the river had taken over, and it was as though her body knew the steps before her mind could catch up. The dance was ancient, older than the village, older than the stars. It was a movement, a rhythm, a flow, a surrender to the forces of the river and the curse that bound her family to it.

Her arms moved in slow arcs, rising and falling like the waves. Her feet shuffled in the water, light but deliberate, as if tracing patterns that had been written into her soul long before she was born. Each motion flowed into the next, a graceful and haunting sequence of movements that felt both foreign and familiar, as though she had been dancing this dance her whole life.

The guardian let out a low growl, its massive body shifting in the water. The light from the cracks in the stone flickered, casting strange shadows on the surface. Amara's eyes were closed now, her mind lost in the rhythm of the dance, but she could feel the creature's eyes on her. She could feel the weight of its presence, the immense power it exuded, and she knew it was watching, waiting, its hunger growing.

Her breath was shallow, her chest rising and falling with the tempo of the dance. Every movement was a prayer. Every step was a promise. To the river. To her ancestors. To the dark force that was pulling her in.

The figure was still standing at the edge of the stone, their gaze fixed on her. "You are doing well," they murmured, their voice barely above a whisper. "But do not forget, Amara. The river never forgets."

Amara didn't understand. She didn't know what she was doing or why. But something deep inside her, buried beneath years of doubt and fear, had risen up in response to the call of the river. She felt it now—its grip on her, tightening, claiming her as its own.

As she danced, the water around her began to shift, ripples spreading outward, matching her every movement. The surface of the river seemed to come alive, swirling with the force of her steps. It was as if the entire river had become her partner, its movements a mirror of her own, guiding her deeper into the unknown.

Nnamdi's voice reached her again, desperate this time. "Amara! Stop! Please!"

But she couldn't stop. She couldn't tear herself away from the rhythm, from the pulse that had taken hold of her. Her movements were fluid, effortless, and she was no longer fully in control of her body. The dance had become a part of her, a connection to the very essence of the river, of the curse that ran through her veins.

The guardian let out another growl, this one louder, more insistent. Its body was rising higher in the water, its claws slicing through the surface as it began to approach. Amara could feel it now—the river was reacting to her. It was testing her, judging her.

A final, trembling note echoed in her chest, and for the first time, she felt the weight of the river's power bear down on her. It was overwhelming, suffocating, and she was no longer sure if she was dancing with the river... or if the river was dancing with her.

Her heart pounded in her ears, her breaths quickening, and the world around her began to twist, the edges of her vision blurring as the guardian closed in. The river was no longer just a body of water; it had become an extension of herself, an entity that demanded everything. Her blood. Her soul. Her very essence.

Amara's final step took her to the edge of the stone, her feet sinking into the water, and the river's pulse reached its crescendo. In that moment, the power of the dance surged through her. She felt her body begin to tremble, her mind stretching to its limits. And then, with a final, aching cry, the river seemed to explode around her, the guardian's roar mingling with the rush of the water.

Everything went silent.

And Amara stood, frozen, at the heart of the river, knowing that nothing—nothing at all—could ever be the same again.

9

The Whispered Warning

Amara stood motionless at the edge of the stone, the cold river lapping at her feet. The dance had ended, or perhaps it had never truly begun. The world around her had fallen eerily silent, the heavy weight of the river's pulse receding as if the water itself had exhaled in relief. Her heart hammered in her chest, her breath coming in shallow, quick bursts, but her body felt distant, as though it no longer belonged to her.

The guardian, once a looming, threatening presence in the water, had disappeared into the depths, vanishing as quickly as it had appeared. The river, too, had quieted, its surface now still, almost unnaturally so. The air felt thick with an unspoken promise—an unsettling calm before the storm.

Behind her, Nnamdi called out her name, his voice sharp with fear, "Amara! Amara, what's happening? Are you—are you okay?"

She didn't respond immediately. Her mind was still tangled in the web of the river's pull, her senses overloaded by the strange, otherworldly connection she had felt during the dance. The rhythm of it, the power of it, the way it had taken control of her body... it was still echoing through her, reverberating in the very marrow of her bones.

"Amara!" Nnamdi's voice broke through her thoughts, urgent now. "You're scaring me!"

She blinked, slowly turning to face him, her eyes unfocused, her gaze distant. He was standing a few feet away, his face pale with worry, his hands trembling at his sides. There was a look in his eyes—fear, yes, but also something else. Something deeper. Something she couldn't quite place.

"I... I'm fine," she said, her voice hoarse, the words coming out slower than she intended. She looked down at her hands, still shaking, the faint marks of the stone's cold surface imprinted on her skin. "It's over."

Nnamdi shook his head, stepping closer, his eyes never leaving her. "What did you do, Amara? What was that? The river... it felt different. Alive, like it was... watching us."

She didn't answer right away. The words of the mysterious figure echoed in her mind, the cryptic warnings they had left her with. *The river never forgets. It has already begun.* She felt something stirring deep within her, a sense of dread that she couldn't shake, a gnawing feeling in her gut that whatever had happened tonight had set something in motion—something irreversible.

"I don't know," she whispered, her voice barely audible over the distant rustling of the trees. She turned away from Nnamdi, her gaze drawn once more to the river, to the stillness that had replaced the chaos. The stone, cracked and glowing, was silent now, its energy no longer pulsing through her. But she could feel its remnants, lingering in her skin like a cold flame.

And then, from the depths of the water, it came.

A voice.

Low. Whispered. Almost indistinguishable from the wind.

"You are marked now."

Amara's breath hitched in her throat. The voice wasn't Nnamdi's, nor was it the figure's. It wasn't even human. It was as though the river itself was speaking to her—its ancient, ageless voice threading through her thoughts like a secret only she could hear.

"Did you hear that?" she asked, her voice trembling. Her eyes darted around, scanning the still surface of the river. The faint glow of the broken stone was the only light, casting long shadows that seemed to shift in the corners of her vision.

Nnamdi's brow furrowed in confusion. "Hear what? Amara, you're scaring me." He reached out to her, his fingers brushing her arm, but she jerked back, suddenly aware of the cold that had crept into her skin, the chill that wasn't just from the night air.

"You are marked."

The voice was louder now, more insistent, reverberating in her chest, in her very bones. She felt a pulse of cold fear wash over her, sinking deep into her heart. Her legs shook, and she stumbled backward, her breath ragged.

"Amara?" Nnamdi's voice broke through, full of concern, but she barely heard him. The world around her was closing in, the shadows lengthening as though the night itself was stretching to claim her. She was drowning in the voice, in the warnings, in the feeling that something terrible was lurking just beneath the surface, waiting to claim her.

The river was alive. It had been watching her. And now it had spoken her name.

"You are marked now."

Her vision blurred as the whispers continued, echoing in her mind, rising to a crescendo. The words tangled together, a single, sinister message. And then, just as abruptly as it had begun, the voice was gone.

For a moment, everything was still.

Amara gasped for air, her body trembling violently. She blinked rapidly, her eyes darting to Nnamdi, who was now standing at a distance, his hands raised, his face pale with alarm. "Amara, talk to me. What's going on? You're scaring me."

She opened her mouth to speak, but her throat felt tight, constricted. The words wouldn't come. It was as if the river had stolen her voice, taken it with the promise of the curse it had now placed upon her.

The wind shifted, carrying with it the faintest whisper, so quiet that it was almost lost in the rustling of the trees. Amara strained to listen, leaning forward, trying to make sense of it.

"Do not trust the river. It has plans for you."

Her blood ran cold. She stumbled back, away from the water, away from the stone, as if to put as much distance as possible between herself and whatever it was that was speaking to her. She could still feel its presence—feel its ancient, malevolent gaze upon her.

Nnamdi's eyes were wide with confusion and growing fear. "Amara, what is it? What's happening to you?"

She shook her head, her voice a hoarse whisper. "The river... it's... it's alive, Nnamdi. It's *aware* of me. It knows me."

A sudden wind gust swept through the clearing, sending a shiver down Amara's spine. The trees around them groaned in protest, and the river rippled violently, as if stirred by something unseen. The whispers had grown stronger, more insistent, and Amara's mind was racing. What had she done? What had she unleashed?

"Amara, you're not making sense. We need to go—" Nnamdi started, but his words were cut off by a sudden, bone-chilling howl that echoed from the depths of the river. It was not an animal's cry. It was the voice of the river itself, the sound of something ancient and furious, something that had been disturbed.

Amara's eyes snapped to the water, her heart leaping into her throat as the surface began to ripple, the calm shattered by the dark, malevolent force rising from below. The guardian, or something like it, was coming back.

The whispers grew louder, mingling with the roar of the water. *"You have awakened it. And now, it will never leave you."*

Nnamdi grabbed her arm, his grip tight with fear. "Amara, we need to go. We need to leave now!"

But Amara could barely hear him. The river had spoken. It had marked her. And the warning was clear: there would be no escape.

The guardian was coming, and with it, the weight of everything she had unleashed.

Amara's blood ran cold, and in that moment, she realized: it wasn't just the river that had been watching her.

It was something far older. Something far darker. And now, it had claimed her.

10

The Hidden Path

The moon hung low in the sky, casting a silver veil over the village. Its pale light flickered through the canopy of trees, dappling the dirt path that led into the heart of the forest. Amara stood at the edge of the forest, the air around her thick with the scent of damp earth and the hum of hidden life. Nnamdi was beside her, his face drawn tight with worry, his eyes scanning the shadows.

"I don't like this," Nnamdi muttered, his voice barely above a whisper. "We shouldn't be out here. We should've gone back to the village, Amara. The river... it's not just water anymore. It's something else."

Amara could feel the weight of his words pressing down on her, but she couldn't bring herself to speak. The river had marked her. The voice, the whispers—everything she had experienced felt like a dream, yet the echoes of it were all too real, pulsing through her veins. She could still hear the guardian's growls in her mind, feel the pull of the water, its icy touch, beckoning her back. There was no denying it—whatever had begun that night had set something irreversible in motion. She could not run from it.

"We have to keep going," she said, her voice firmer than she felt. Her eyes were drawn to the dark shadows beyond the path, to the thick forest that had always seemed so familiar yet now seemed like a place of secrets—hidden places she had never noticed before. Places she now feared.

"But the forest..." Nnamdi's voice trembled with doubt. "There are stories, Amara. The elders—"

"I know," she interrupted, her gaze hardening. "I know the stories. But we don't have a choice." She turned to face him fully now, her eyes locking with his. "If I'm going to find out what's really happening, if I'm going to stop this—whatever this is—I need to follow the path. The one they warned us about."

For a long moment, Nnamdi said nothing. His expression was unreadable, his lips pressed tightly together. But after a moment, he sighed, defeated, and nodded. "Fine. But I don't like this. I don't like any of it."

With that, they stepped off the well-worn path and into the forest. The trees were taller here, their branches stretching high above them, creating a canopy that blocked out much of the moonlight. The air was thick with moisture, and the ground beneath their feet was soft, giving slightly with each step. The quiet was suffocating, as if the forest itself was holding its breath.

Amara's heart pounded in her chest as they walked, each step deeper into the woods feeling like a step away from everything she knew. She could feel the weight of the ancient trees around them, their presence heavy and watching. She was aware of the way the shadows seemed to shift as they moved, the rustle of leaves whispering secrets just beyond her hearing. The forest was alive, and it seemed to be paying attention to them.

The path ahead was barely visible, a faint trail winding through the underbrush, marked only by the occasional flicker of moonlight on the uneven ground. But something in Amara's chest urged her forward, an instinct that had awakened within her ever since the night by the river. She didn't know why, but she had the feeling that the answers she sought were hidden somewhere within the depths of the forest.

"What if it's just a legend?" Nnamdi asked, his voice a little less certain now, as if the eerie quiet of the woods was starting to unsettle him. "What if there's nothing here? No path, no... nothing?"

Amara shook her head, her jaw tightening. "It's not a legend. It's real. I can feel it."

They walked in silence for a while, the only sound the crunch of dried leaves underfoot and the occasional rustle of animals moving unseen through the brush. The deeper they ventured, the more the forest seemed to close in around them. The trees grew thicker, their trunks twisting in strange shapes, their roots rising above the ground in knotted tangles.

And then, just as Amara was beginning to doubt her instincts, she saw it—a narrow opening in the trees, barely noticeable, as if it had been waiting for her all along. The path was hidden, tucked away between the gnarled roots of an ancient tree, its bark thick and weathered by time. It seemed to beckon to her, the shadows around it shifting in a way that made her skin prickle.

She stopped. "This is it," she said quietly.

Nnamdi followed her gaze, his eyes wide with unease. "Amara, no. We can't go in there."

But Amara could already feel the pull of the path, the way it seemed to call to her. There was no turning back now. She stepped forward, her foot brushing against the moss-covered stones that marked the entrance. The air grew colder, and for a brief moment, she thought she heard a whisper, low and hissing, as if the trees themselves were speaking to her.

"You are too late."

Amara froze, her breath catching in her throat. The whisper was faint, almost imperceptible, but it was there—clear as day. It was the river's voice, distant and cold. Her heart raced as she glanced at Nnamdi, who was looking at her with wide, terrified eyes.

"We have to keep going," she whispered, more to herself than to him. She didn't understand why, but the words felt like they came from somewhere deep within, a command she had no choice but to follow.

Reluctantly, Nnamdi took a step forward, then another, and before long, they were both stepping through the hidden entrance, into the unknown.

The path wound in a gentle curve, leading them further into the forest's depths. The air grew denser, and the silence seemed to press in on them, suffocating in its intensity. The shadows were deeper here, darker, and the feeling of being watched only intensified. The trees towered above them like ancient sentinels, their branches tangled and reaching out as if to trap them.

Amara's pulse quickened with every step, but she pressed on, her mind racing with thoughts of what awaited them. The forest felt alive, but not in a comforting way. It was as if the woods themselves were keeping secrets—secrets that had been buried for centuries.

The path took them in a circle, weaving between trees and thick underbrush, until Amara could no longer tell which direction they had come from. She turned to Nnamdi, but he was staring straight ahead, his face pale and drawn.

"We're lost," he said, his voice trembling. "This path—it's changing. It's—"

Before he could finish, a low rumble echoed through the trees, a sound like the earth itself groaning beneath their feet. The air seemed to thicken, and Amara felt an icy chill settle over her. Her skin prickled, and she instinctively reached out for Nnamdi's hand.

"We need to turn back," he said urgently. "This is wrong. We shouldn't be here."

But Amara wasn't listening. The whispers had returned, louder this time, swirling around her like a storm. She stepped forward, her eyes narrowing as she saw a faint glow ahead. It was weak at first, but as they drew closer, it grew stronger, illuminating the path before them.

And then, in the clearing ahead, she saw it.

A stone circle, ancient and worn by time, its surface etched with symbols she didn't recognize. The ground within the circle was bare, save for a small, glimmering pool of water at the center, reflecting the pale moonlight like a mirror.

Amara's heart skipped a beat. She knew, somehow, that this was what she had been searching for. This was the heart of the forest—the place that held the answers. And yet, as she stepped closer, she felt a sense of dread wash over her, a deep, unshakable fear that warned her not to get too close.

The pool seemed to ripple, even though there was no wind. And then, just as she reached out to touch it, a voice—low and trembling—whispered from the darkness.

"You shouldn't have come."

Amara froze, her hand hovering over the water. The voice was familiar, but distorted, like the echo of something long buried.

Behind her, the shadows seemed to stir.

Something was watching.

And it was too late to turn back.

11

The Silent Promise

Amara's heart raced as the voice echoed through the clearing, chilling her to the bone. The words lingered in the air, suspended between the trees, until the very ground beneath her seemed to vibrate with their presence. *"You shouldn't have come."* The voice wasn't loud, but it carried an unbearable weight, like the final breath of a dying wind, mournful and inevitable. It was a voice that seemed to come from everywhere—and nowhere—at once, rising from the depths of the forest like a hidden secret.

She didn't move, her hand still hovering inches above the rippling water in the center of the stone circle. The pool had grown darker, its surface no longer reflecting the moonlight but instead seeming to swallow it whole, absorbing every last trace of light. A thick, unnatural silence had fallen over the forest, more oppressive than the darkness itself.

Behind her, she could hear Nnamdi's shallow breathing, his footsteps tentative as he stepped closer, but she couldn't tear her gaze away from the pool. It felt as if something was waiting beneath the surface—something ancient and powerful, waiting for her to make the wrong move.

"Amara..." Nnamdi's voice was tight, fragile. "We should go. Now. This place... it's wrong. It feels wrong."

Amara felt his hand on her shoulder, gentle but insistent, pulling her away from the edge of the stone circle. But she couldn't look away. Something deep inside her—the same instinct that had driven her into the forest in the first place—was urging her to stay, to find the answers, no matter the cost.

The whispers had stopped, and the forest had fallen eerily still, as though holding its breath in anticipation. She took a step forward, ignoring the panic that was beginning to rise in Nnamdi's voice, the way his fingers tightened around her arm.

"Please, Amara," he said, desperation creeping into his tone. "We're too deep in. Whatever's in there—it's not for us. It's not meant for people like us."

Amara turned her head slowly, her eyes locking with his. For the first time since they'd entered the forest, she saw the fear in his eyes—real, raw fear. She knew he wasn't just scared for himself. He was scared for her, too. And the truth was, she wasn't sure what was more terrifying: the forest, or the feeling that something was pulling her toward it—toward the pool, toward the answers she was beginning to understand, answers that were far darker than she had ever imagined.

"I have to know, Nnamdi," she said softly, her voice barely audible over the pulse of her own heartbeat. "I have to find out what's happening to me."

Nnamdi's grip on her arm tightened, his face pleading. "Please, Amara. Don't do this. Whatever you're feeling—it's not real. It's the forest playing tricks on you. It's the river. It's—"

The words died in his throat as a low rumble resonated from deep within the earth. The ground beneath them trembled, and the trees around them groaned as if the entire forest was waking from a long slumber. Amara turned back to the pool, her eyes drawn once again to the swirling darkness beneath the surface. The ripples began to spread outward, moving in unnatural, rhythmic patterns, like something stirring from the depths.

And then, as if summoned by the sound, a figure rose from the water.

It was not human. Not entirely.

At first, Amara thought it was a reflection, some strange trick of the light. But no—the figure was real, its form rising slowly from the pool, twisting as though emerging from a place far darker than the world above. Its body was a shifting mass of shadows and light, its edges blurred, as if it could not quite maintain its shape. There was a gleaming, otherworldly shine to it, like moonlight trapped in liquid.

It was... *something*—something ancient. Something that had been buried beneath the earth and the river for centuries, waiting. Watching.

Amara's breath caught in her throat as the figure took shape, its eyes glowing with an eerie, unnatural light. The creature's features were vaguely human, but its skin shimmered with iridescent scales, and its limbs seemed to stretch and distort, a grotesque imitation of life. It was beautiful and terrifying at once, a being that defied reason.

The creature's gaze fell on Amara, and in that instant, she felt its presence like a heavy weight pressing down on her chest. Her breath hitched, her heart racing as if it were trying to escape her body. She could feel the creature's power—its coldness—flowing through her veins, sending chills down her spine. The whispers returned, louder now, a chorus of voices rising from the depths of the pool, calling to her, beckoning her closer.

"*You are the one... the chosen one...*" The voice was soft but firm, like the echo of a forgotten prophecy. "*The promise was made long ago... now you must fulfill it.*"

Amara's mind spun. Chosen? Promise? What did this creature mean? What had been promised? Her knees felt weak, and for a moment, she thought she might collapse. But she couldn't move. Couldn't look away.

Nnamdi's grip on her arm tightened, his panic palpable. "Amara! Please—let's go! This isn't you! Don't listen to it!"

But Amara barely heard him. She was drowning in the creature's gaze, the force of its presence overwhelming her, drowning out everything else. She could feel its power, its ancient knowledge, rising within her, taking root deep in her soul.

"It is too late," the creature continued, its voice reverberating in her chest. *"The path has already been set. The river has chosen. And you are bound to it, just as the promise was bound to you."*

The words were like a weight pressing down on her chest, suffocating her. She wanted to scream, to fight back, but she couldn't move. It felt as though the forest, the creature, and the river had conspired to trap her here, in this moment, and she had no choice but to listen.

For a brief, terrifying moment, she wondered if she was losing herself entirely. If she was becoming something else—something that didn't belong to the world she had known. Her mind flashed to the river's voice, to the cryptic warnings, to the cold touch of the water on her skin. The same feeling—power, fear, and an undeniable sense of inevitability—had gripped her then, too.

And then, as though in answer to her silent plea, the creature's gaze softened, its expression shifting into something almost... affectionate. It reached a long, gnarled hand toward her, the fingers impossibly long, each one tipped with something that gleamed like metal in the moonlight.

"It was promised," it whispered. *"The cycle is complete. You have awakened the river. And now... now you must claim your inheritance."*

Amara's chest tightened as the words hit her. Inheritance. What inheritance? What had she done? What had she awakened?

The creature's eyes never left hers, and for a brief, terrifying moment, she felt a deep connection with it—as though its ancient power was woven into her very being. There was no turning back now. The promise had been made. The path was set.

And she was the one who had to walk it.

Without a word, the creature lowered its hand, and the water in the pool began to swirl violently, as if stirred by an invisible current. Amara's heart skipped a beat, her pulse racing as the air around them seemed to thicken.

This was it. She was at the center of something far bigger than herself, something that had been unfolding for centuries. The promise, the inheritance, the river—it was all connected. And now, it was hers to claim.

Nnamdi's voice broke through her thoughts, frantic and urgent. "Amara! Don't—"

But before he could finish, the creature's eyes flickered toward him, and a deep growl rumbled from within its throat.

"*Leave.*" The voice was a command, an order that left no room for argument.

Amara turned her head slowly to look at Nnamdi. His face was pale with fear, his eyes wide with panic. He opened his mouth to speak, but the creature's voice silenced him.

And just like that, Amara knew what she had to do.

The promise had been made.

Now, there was no turning back.

12

The Ghost's Visit

The night pressed down upon the forest like a heavy cloak, suffocating and thick with the weight of unspeakable things. The air was still, save for the occasional rustling of unseen creatures in the underbrush. Amara stood at the edge of the stone circle, the moonlight barely filtering through the canopy, casting long, twisted shadows on the ground. Nnamdi's frantic breath was the only sound beside the pounding of her own heart, the rhythm of it echoing in her ears, too loud, too fast.

"Amara... please..." Nnamdi's voice was barely a whisper, laced with a fear she had never heard from him before. He stood just behind her, his hand gripping her arm so tightly it almost hurt, as though he could stop her from doing something he couldn't understand.

But Amara didn't turn to face him. She couldn't. Her eyes were locked on the pool—the dark, swirling water that seemed to pulse with a life of its own. The creature had retreated back into its shadowy form, its body a shifting mass of darkness, still hovering just above the surface of the water. It was watching her with those glowing eyes, and Amara could feel its gaze piercing her very soul.

Inheritance, it had said.

The word echoed in her mind like a curse. What did it mean? What had she inherited? And why her? Why now?

Her skin tingled, the sensation of something watching her growing sharper with every passing second. There was a presence here, something beyond the creature in the pool, something older, colder. The trees around them groaned, their limbs swaying as if in response to some invisible force. The wind began to stir, a low, mournful sound rising from the forest floor.

And then, in the distance, a figure appeared.

At first, Amara thought it was another trick of the forest, a shadow drifting between the trees, but as the figure came closer, the air around her grew heavier, colder. The temperature dropped, and her breath turned to mist before her eyes. The darkness seemed to part around the figure as it emerged from the trees—a tall, slender form, draped in tattered robes that fluttered even though there was no wind. It moved soundlessly, its feet not quite touching the ground, as though it were gliding, its presence filling the clearing with an oppressive silence.

Amara froze, her pulse quickening as the figure came into full view. The face was pale, almost translucent, its features soft and indistinct, like a reflection on water that was slowly fading. But there was something about the eyes—two dark, hollow pits where eyes should have been, deep and endless, like a void that pulled at her soul. The figure's gaze was fixed on her, and in that moment, Amara knew—this was no mere phantom of the forest.

This was a ghost.

A cold chill wrapped itself around Amara's chest, squeezing the air from her lungs. She could hear Nnamdi's breath catch behind her, but the sound was muffled, as though he were a world away. The ghost moved closer, its robes flowing around it like the mist, and Amara felt an overwhelming pressure in the air. It was as if the very forest itself had fallen silent, holding its breath in anticipation.

"Who... who are you?" Amara's voice trembled, the words barely escaping her throat. She felt a sharp, sudden pain in her chest, a pressure that made her knees buckle. The ghost's presence was suffocating, its very being pressing down on her like a weight she couldn't escape.

The ghost did not answer immediately. It merely tilted its head, as though studying her, its dark, hollow eyes never leaving her face. For a moment, time seemed to stretch, the forest holding its breath, the entire world frozen in place.

Then, the voice came. It was a whisper, barely audible, like the rustling of dry leaves, but it carried the weight of centuries.

"You are not meant to be here," it said, its voice soft but laced with sorrow. The words seemed to echo in the air, reverberating through Amara's bones. *"This place... this path, this inheritance—none of it was meant for you."*

Amara's heart thudded painfully in her chest. "What do you mean? I don't understand."

The ghost took a step forward, its form flickering as if the air itself was bending around it. It reached out with a long, ethereal hand, its fingers unnaturally long, the skin almost translucent, and placed it gently on her forehead. A cold, unyielding sensation spread through her body, as though ice had been poured into her veins. Amara gasped, her whole body seizing as the touch seemed to invade her very mind.

Memories—visions—flashed before her eyes, sharp and disjointed. She saw a river, vast and dark, stretching beyond the horizon. She saw people, their faces twisted in fear and longing. There were shadows—figures cloaked in mist, moving between trees that whispered their secrets to the wind. The river roared, its waters swallowing everything in its path, drowning the land, drowning the people. And in the midst of it all, there was a woman—a woman who looked like her, but older, and with eyes that burned with a fire that could not be extinguished.

Amara recoiled, pulling away from the ghost's touch, her breath ragged. The images faded, leaving her dizzy and disoriented, as though the world had shifted beneath her feet. The ghost was still standing before her, its face unreadable, the air around it thick with grief and something darker, something older than time itself.

"You do not know what you have awakened," the ghost whispered, its voice laden with an ancient sorrow. *"The river has chosen... but it is not for you to control. You cannot escape what was set in motion long ago."*

THE GHOST'S VISIT

Amara's mind raced, her chest tightening with a panic she couldn't explain. The ghost's words hung in the air, heavy with meaning, and yet she couldn't understand them fully. *The river has chosen.* She had felt it, the pull of something beyond the mortal world, something that had latched onto her. But why? Why her?

The ghost's hollow eyes seemed to pierce through her, reading the very depths of her soul. *"You are bound to it now,"* it whispered. *"Bound to the river. Bound to the promise. And there is no escaping your fate."*

The words sent a shiver down Amara's spine, a coldness settling deep in her bones. A fate? What fate? Was the promise the river had spoken of all that she was now destined for? Was there truly no turning back?

The ghost lingered, its presence like a shadow that had settled over her very soul, its words sinking deep into her thoughts. For a moment, the world seemed to pause, the only sound the soft rustling of the leaves in the distance. Then, without another word, the ghost began to fade, its form dissolving into the mist, as though it had never been there at all.

Amara's breath came in short, shallow gasps. She was alone once more in the clearing, the air thick with the ghost's words, and the oppressive weight of the forest closing in around her. The figure, the haunting presence—it was gone. But the fear, the unanswered questions, the sense of an unrelenting pull toward something darker—those remained.

She turned to Nnamdi, who was still standing a few feet behind her, his face pale and drawn with terror. His eyes locked with hers, wide with disbelief.

"Amara..." he whispered, his voice trembling. "What... what was that?"

Amara didn't know. She didn't have the answers, but she could feel them coming. The ghost had spoken of a promise, of a fate bound to her, and the river's unyielding choice. It was all connected. She could feel the weight of it in her chest, like a ticking clock, counting down the moments to something inevitable.

The ghost's visit had left her with more questions than answers. But one thing was clear: there was no escape from the path she had set upon. The river, the inheritance, the promise—it was all part of something much larger than she could comprehend. And there was no turning back now.

With a final, lingering glance at the darkened pool, Amara turned and began to walk away, the weight of the ghost's words pressing down on her like a shadow that would never lift.

The path ahead was uncertain, but the journey had only just begun.

13

The Broken Trust

The wind howled through the trees as Amara trudged back through the forest, her thoughts a chaotic blur. Her heart pounded in her chest, a steady drumbeat of fear and confusion, every step a reminder that nothing in her world was as it seemed. The ghost's visit, the promises, the inheritance, and the whispers of the river all tangled in her mind, leaving her with a sense of dread so deep it threatened to swallow her whole.

Behind her, Nnamdi's hurried footsteps followed, his presence a constant reminder of the tension that had gripped them both since they had entered the forest. She could feel his eyes on her, could almost hear the questions he wanted to ask but could never bring himself to say. The forest felt alive tonight, but not in the way it usually did—this time, it was watching them, as if the trees themselves had ears, listening to their every word, to their every thought.

"I don't understand, Amara," Nnamdi's voice broke through the silence, strained and soft. "What did that thing want? What did it mean when it said you were 'bound to it'? What is this inheritance it keeps talking about?"

Amara's breath caught in her throat, and she felt the weight of his words settle on her shoulders. She wanted to tell him everything—wanted to explain it all, make sense of the chaos swirling in her mind—but the truth was, she didn't understand it herself. She only knew that something had been set in motion, something too big to stop.

The promise made, the river's call—it all led back to her, and now she was bound to it in ways she couldn't escape.

"I don't know, Nnamdi," she said, her voice barely a whisper. "But I feel it. The river... it's calling to me. And I can't ignore it. No matter how much I want to."

He was silent behind her, and for a moment, Amara wondered if he understood, or if he was simply afraid of what she was becoming. She couldn't blame him. The path she was walking—had walked into—was dark and filled with danger. And yet, something in her could not turn away.

The moon was full overhead, its light casting long shadows on the ground, the silver rays dancing on the forest floor like ghosts. They were close now to the edge of the forest, where the path split—the trail that led to the village, and the one that veered deeper into the wildlands, toward the river.

Amara stopped abruptly, her heart leaping into her throat. Something was wrong. She could feel it—the air had changed, the heavy stillness replaced by an unnerving tension. The forest had gone silent, the usual sounds of night creatures stilled. She could hear only her own breathing, Nnamdi's breathing, and then—

A rustle.

It was barely perceptible, but Amara heard it—like the sound of someone shifting through the underbrush, trying to stay hidden. Her body went rigid. She turned quickly to Nnamdi, her hand instinctively reaching for him, but he was already stepping forward, his face tight with unease.

"You feel it too, don't you?" Nnamdi whispered, his voice tinged with fear.

Before Amara could respond, a figure emerged from the shadows at the edge of the clearing.

At first, it was only a silhouette, tall and indistinct, but as it stepped into the light of the moon, Amara's breath caught in her throat. The figure was familiar—too familiar. It was a man, tall and broad-shouldered, his face half-hidden beneath a hooded cloak. But it wasn't just any man. It was Eze, the village elder—the same man who had warned her away from the river days before, the one who had spoken in riddles about fate and promises.

But now, his presence was different, darker. The smile that had once been warm and reassuring was gone, replaced by something colder, more calculating. He stood in the clearing as if he owned it, his gaze fixed directly on Amara, as though he were waiting for something.

"Nnamdi," Eze's voice was low, almost too calm, "I thought you would have learned by now to listen to your elders."

Nnamdi stepped in front of Amara instinctively, his body tense with readiness. "What do you want, Eze?" His voice was sharp, full of suspicion. "You're the one who told us to stay away from this place. So why are you here?"

Eze's lips curled into a smile, but it didn't reach his eyes. "I'm not here to stop you, Nnamdi. I'm here for Amara."

Amara felt her blood run cold. The air around her seemed to freeze as his words hung in the air. She took a step back, instinctively moving toward Nnamdi, but the elder didn't seem concerned by her actions. Instead, he stepped forward, his eyes never leaving hers.

"Amara," Eze said softly, his voice oddly soothing, "you've been given a gift. A gift that will change everything. But you don't understand it yet. You don't see the truth of it."

The words sent a shiver down her spine. She had heard them before—the ghost's whisper, the river's call. But from Eze, they were something different. Something more dangerous. His voice was not just soft, but insistent, drawing her in, like a spider luring its prey into the web.

"I don't want your gift," Amara said, her voice shaking. She couldn't let him manipulate her the way he had manipulated the others. "I don't want anything to do with the river. I don't care about the promises or the inheritance. I want to leave."

Eze's expression softened, but there was no warmth in it. "You have no choice, Amara," he said, the calmness in his tone betraying the urgency in his eyes. "You have already made your choice when you stepped into the river. And now, you're bound to it. The promise is made, the river has claimed you. You are the one who will carry its power."

Amara shook her head, panic rising in her chest. "No. I won't—"

"You will," Eze interrupted, his voice like a whisper in her ear. "The river does not ask for permission. And you cannot run from it, no matter how far you go. It has already decided."

Nnamdi stepped forward, his voice low and protective. "You're lying," he said, his fists clenched. "You've always been lying, Eze. This is about power—about control. You've used Amara to fulfill some twisted plan, haven't you?"

For a moment, Eze's face darkened. The air crackled with an unnatural tension, and Amara felt the weight of the forest closing in around them. The trees seemed to lean in, as though listening to the words between them.

"I have never lied to you, Nnamdi," Eze said, his tone dangerously calm. "But sometimes, the truth is a dangerous thing. And it's not always a truth you want to hear."

Amara's chest tightened. She didn't understand. This was not the Eze she had known—the wise elder who had seemed to care for the village, who had guided her and Nnamdi with the weight of his knowledge. No, this was someone else. Someone who had used her. Used the river. Used the promise.

And in that moment, the truth became clear—Eze had never been their ally. He had never been a protector.

He was part of something much darker, and now, he had come to claim her as part of his twisted game.

The trust she had placed in him—everything she had believed about the river and the promises—had been shattered in an instant.

Amara took a deep breath, her mind racing. She had been fooled. But she wouldn't let him control her any longer. The river's call still echoed in her ears, but now, something else had awakened in her—something that made her realize she had more power than she had ever understood.

The trust was broken. And now, she was going to fight for the truth.

14

The Night of Secrets

The moon hung low in the sky, casting an eerie silver glow over the village. The air was thick with a chill that made every breath feel sharp, as if the night itself were cutting into her skin. Amara stood alone in the small clearing behind the elder's hut, her eyes fixed on the distant horizon where the river wound through the land, dark and unpredictable. Her heart was a wild drumbeat in her chest, each thud a reminder of the secrets she had uncovered—and the ones still hidden from her.

Nnamdi had left her not long ago, his words still echoing in her ears, full of uncertainty and fear. "You have to be careful, Amara," he had warned. "The more you search for answers, the more dangerous this becomes."

But Amara wasn't afraid anymore. The weight of the broken trust had transformed something in her—something deep inside. She could feel it, that unexplainable pull, that connection to the river, to the promise made, to the power that was now inside her. The ghost's words had haunted her, but they had also awoken something she couldn't ignore. She was a part of this story, whether she liked it or not.

A rustle behind her made her spin around, her breath catching in her throat. It was just the wind. Or maybe it wasn't. She wasn't sure anymore.

The forest had been too quiet lately, too still. Even the animals had gone silent, leaving her to wonder if something—someone—was watching her. The ghost had said the river had chosen, and now, she understood that whatever was coming, she couldn't escape it. Not now. Not ever.

She took a deep breath and stepped forward, her feet crunching softly against the dirt path. She couldn't ignore the pull any longer. The time had come to face what she had been avoiding—the truth buried deep within the village, under layers of secrecy and silence. Tonight, she would learn everything.

The village itself seemed to hold its breath as she made her way through the winding streets, the shadows of the huts looming like dark sentinels in the night. The occasional flicker of a lantern light through a window was the only sign of life, and the air around her was thick with tension, as if the earth itself was aware of her purpose.

She reached the small square in front of the elders' gathering hall, the largest hut in the village. It stood in the center, like a throne, ancient and imposing. The walls were marked with faded carvings of forgotten symbols—symbols she'd seen in her dreams but never fully understood. Now, standing before them, they felt alive. Watching her. Waiting.

"Amara."

The voice came from behind her, so soft that it was barely a whisper, yet it froze her in place. She turned, her eyes widening as she faced the figure emerging from the shadows. It was Eze—the village elder. But this was not the same man she had encountered before. His face was darker, his eyes sunken with exhaustion, as though something had drained the life from him. He looked older now, more weathered, the weight of his secrets pulling him down.

"Eze," Amara said, her voice tight. "What are you doing here? I thought I told you—"

"I know what you thought," he interrupted, his voice low and grave. "But you don't understand, child. You think you're seeking the truth, but the truth is far more dangerous than you realize."

Amara's heart beat faster, her hands trembling slightly. "What do you mean?" She took a cautious step forward, her mind reeling from his words. "What's so dangerous about the truth?"

Eze took a slow, deliberate step toward her, his eyes narrowing as if searching for something inside her. "There are things you don't know. Things you were never meant to know. Things buried so deep, only the river can reveal them. But once you've seen it, once you understand what is hidden beneath the surface, there's no going back."

Amara's throat tightened, a cold sweat forming on her brow. His words—his warning—rang in her ears like a distant bell. But still, she felt herself drawn to the mystery, to the answers she so desperately sought.

"I have to know," she said, her voice barely above a whisper. "I have to understand."

Eze's lips curled into a grim smile, but it wasn't one of reassurance. It was something darker, like the calm before a storm. "Very well," he said, his voice cold and steady. "Come with me."

Without another word, he turned and walked toward the elder's hall, and Amara followed, her steps hesitant but determined. The doors of the hall creaked open with an unsettling groan as Eze led her inside, where the air was thick with the scent of old incense and the faint trace of something metallic. The shadows inside the hall seemed to stretch and twist unnaturally, as if the walls themselves were alive.

Inside, the hall was dim, the only light coming from the flickering candles placed in corners of the room. The walls were adorned with intricate carvings—more symbols, more forgotten lore. But it was the center of the room that drew her attention. There, in the middle of the floor, was an altar, ancient and weathered, its surface covered with a layer of dust. And on the altar lay a large, ornate stone—a stone she had seen before.

It was the same stone she had found at the river's edge.

Amara's breath caught in her throat as she stepped closer. The stone was warm to the touch, its surface smooth and polished, though the markings on it were faded and almost indecipherable.

"You recognize it," Eze said, his voice soft but insistent. "This is where it all began, Amara. This stone, this altar—it holds the key to everything. The river, the inheritance, the promise… It's all tied to this. And to you."

She felt the weight of his words settle in her chest like a stone, heavier than anything she had ever felt. "What do you mean?" she asked, her voice cracking. "Why me?"

Eze's eyes locked onto hers, dark and knowing. "Because you were born for it. Born to carry it. The river chose you, Amara. You are the one who must unlock its secrets. And once you do, there will be no turning back."

He gestured to the stone. "The truth is in this stone. But only if you are willing to see it."

Amara swallowed hard, her mind racing. The weight of the moment pressed on her like a physical force, as if the very air had thickened with the weight of untold secrets.

"I'm ready," she said, though the words felt hollow, as if she were lying to herself. She reached out, her fingers trembling as they brushed the surface of the stone.

The instant her skin touched it, a searing heat shot through her, sharp and unyielding. The stone pulsed beneath her fingertips, sending a shockwave through her body. The world seemed to tilt, spinning in a dizzying blur. And then, in the blink of an eye, everything changed.

Visions flooded her mind—snapshots of moments long past, of shadows moving in the night, of the river surging and consuming. Faces twisted in agony, cries of despair filling the air. And then, the figure of a woman, standing in the heart of the river, her eyes empty, her expression cold. It was the woman from the ghost's vision—the one who looked like Amara, but older.

A voice whispered in her mind, so faint at first she thought it was her imagination.

The river calls to you. It always has.

Amara gasped, pulling her hand away from the stone, her heart racing, her breath coming in ragged gasps. She stumbled back, nearly losing her balance.

"What was that?" she gasped, her voice trembling.

Eze's eyes gleamed, almost with satisfaction. "The beginning of the end, child. You've seen it now. You've touched it."

The room seemed to close in on her, the air heavy with the weight of what she had just learned, and what she still didn't understand.

"Now, you know," Eze whispered. "The truth has been revealed. But remember this—there is always a cost to the secrets of the river. And for you, Amara, the price has only just begun."

Amara's chest tightened as she tried to comprehend what she had seen, what had been revealed to her. The night had only begun, but already, the shadows seemed deeper, darker, more dangerous. And she realized then, with a sinking dread, that the river was not just a force of nature—it was a force of destiny.

And now, it was hers to face.

15

The Unseen Hand

The world felt different now. The cold that had settled in Amara's bones the moment her fingers touched the stone seemed to have spread deeper, infecting everything around her. She couldn't shake the feeling that the very air had shifted, as though an invisible hand had reached into her life and begun to twist things beyond her control.

Her heart was still pounding from the vision, from the knowledge that she had glimpsed something so powerful, so ancient, that it had broken her sense of reality. The river, the stone, the woman from the ghost's vision—they were all connected to her in ways she didn't fully understand. And now, there was a new force at work, something darker and far more dangerous.

Eze's voice still echoed in her ears. *The price has only just begun.*

She had wanted answers. She had asked for them, demanded them, even. But the truth had come at a cost she wasn't ready to pay. The air around her felt thick, suffocating. She wanted to scream, to run, but something—some unseen force—was holding her in place.

The village was quiet when she stepped outside the elder's hall, the path before her bathed in moonlight. But it wasn't the peaceful kind of silence she had grown accustomed to. This silence was suffocating, oppressive, as if the very earth were holding its breath.

Amara took a hesitant step forward, her eyes darting to the shadows that seemed to move on their own. The trees loomed over her, their branches like skeletal hands reaching out to grasp her, and the wind whispered through them, carrying with it a warning that made her spine tingle.

Behind her, the door to the hall creaked shut with a hollow, final sound. She turned, but no one emerged. Eze was gone.

But she wasn't alone.

It was as though something was moving just out of her sight, flickering at the edges of her vision. A presence. She could feel it in her chest, a pressure that was growing heavier with every passing moment, as if an unseen hand were tightening its grip around her heart.

Her breath caught in her throat. *Who is it?* she thought. *Who's watching me?*

She didn't need to turn around to know the answer. The feeling of being followed—watched—was all too familiar. She had felt it before, back at the river, when the ghost's voice had whispered in her ear. The same eerie sensation of something lurking, just beyond her reach, its intentions unclear. It was the feeling of being trapped, of being pulled into something far bigger than herself.

She spun around quickly, her pulse racing. Nothing. The clearing was empty, the night still.

But then, she heard it—a faint rustling behind her, like someone moving through the underbrush. She froze, her heart hammering in her chest.

"Amara," a voice called softly, so soft it might have been carried on the wind. But she knew who it was.

Eze's voice.

She turned again, but there was no one there. Only shadows.

The wind shifted. A chill rushed over her, colder than before, and she pulled her cloak tighter around her shoulders. Something was wrong. The world felt... wrong. The very fabric of the night was tearing at the seams.

This is not real, she thought desperately. *It can't be.*

But even as the thought formed, something within her—something deep, something dark—began to whisper. *You can feel it, can't you? The truth is inescapable now. You are bound to it. To the river. To me.*

Her blood ran cold. The voice—was it the river? Or was it something else? Something older, more malevolent? She took a step back, the fear seizing her body like a vice, but the unseen force pushed forward. The trees shifted as if alive, the wind howling with sudden violence.

And then, she saw it.

A figure emerged from the shadows, its form barely visible in the darkness. It moved too quickly, too fluidly, as if it were more shadow than flesh. Amara's breath caught in her throat as the figure stepped into the light, revealing the pale, almost translucent skin, the long dark hair cascading down its back. It was the woman from the river. The woman from the vision. Her face was hollow, as if life had been drained from her, and her eyes gleamed with an unsettling intensity—empty and yet so full of rage.

Amara stumbled backward, her legs weak beneath her. "Who are you?" she gasped, her voice barely a whisper.

The woman didn't speak. Instead, she raised her hand, long fingers curling toward Amara in a gesture that felt like a command, like a summons.

Amara's heart skipped a beat as she felt the ground beneath her shift, the earth trembling as if responding to the woman's silent call. The air around her thickened, and the shadows deepened, as if the night itself had come alive, bending to the will of the unseen force.

Without warning, the woman moved closer, her steps impossibly silent, her eyes fixed on Amara with an intensity that made her stomach churn. She was drawn toward the woman, her body moving against her will, as if tethered to the figure by some invisible chain.

"Stop," Amara gasped, struggling against the force that pulled her forward. "What do you want from me?"

The woman's lips parted, but no sound emerged. Her gaze never wavered from Amara's face, her eyes cold and unfeeling. The woman reached out, her fingers brushing lightly against Amara's skin, sending a shockwave of cold through her body. The touch was ice, and Amara shuddered, her knees buckling beneath her.

A voice whispered in her mind again. *You are mine.*

The words froze her blood. She gasped for air, but the weight of them suffocated her.

"No," Amara whispered desperately. "I'm not yours."

But the woman's expression didn't change. Her grip on Amara tightened, her cold fingers digging into her flesh, and for the first time, Amara felt the full force of what she was up against. This was no mere vision. No fleeting ghost. This was something much older. Something that had been waiting, lurking, for her.

She was connected to it. Bound by the river, by the promises made, by the things she had yet to understand. And now, it was coming for her.

The world tilted again, and Amara's vision blurred. She felt herself falling—plummeting, deeper and deeper—until the ground beneath her gave way entirely.

The woman's cold laughter echoed around her, sharp and hollow.

"Fool," she whispered, though her voice was not hers, but something far darker, a voice that made Amara's skin crawl. "You think you are in control? You think you can escape what has already been written?"

Amara's body was no longer her own, her movements guided by the unseen hand that gripped her heart. She could feel it now—the river, the power surging through her veins, the pull of something ancient and primal.

"Let go," the woman whispered, her voice fading, as if swallowed by the wind. "Let go, and join me. You are mine now."

The last thing Amara remembered before everything went black was the river's whisper, louder than ever before, pounding in her ears.

You are mine. Forever.

And then—nothing.

When Amara awoke, she was lying on the ground, the cold earth pressing against her skin. Her body felt heavy, as if it were made of stone. Her eyes fluttered open, but the world around her was blurred, spinning.

The woman was gone.

But the pull was still there, stronger than ever.

The unseen hand had claimed her. And now, there was no turning back.

16

The Darkening Sky

Amara woke with a start, gasping for breath as though she had been underwater. Her heart thundered in her chest, each beat echoing in her ears. Her body was cold, every muscle aching as though she had been frozen in place for hours. She blinked rapidly, trying to make sense of the darkness around her. It was as if the world itself had swallowed her whole—nothing felt real, nothing felt safe.

The air was thick with the scent of damp earth and decay, and her breath came out in visible puffs, the chill creeping deeper into her skin. She sat up slowly, her eyes adjusting to the dim, unfamiliar surroundings. The ground beneath her was soft, muddy, and wet—like she had fallen into some kind of bog. But where was she? How had she gotten here?

The last thing she remembered was the woman—the pale, cold figure who had touched her, and then the feeling of falling, falling into nothing. Her heart skipped a beat as the fragments of the memory pieced together like shards of broken glass.

The woman's voice still echoed in her mind. *You are mine now. Forever.*

Amara shuddered, her hands trembling as she pushed herself up from the muddy ground. Her legs were unsteady, as though they didn't belong to her, her body refusing to cooperate. The cold, the weight of it, was unbearable. The moon above was hidden behind thick clouds, the night sky appearing more like a bruise than a canopy of stars. Something was wrong. The sky was wrong. The air felt like it was closing in on her.

She stood, her body swaying slightly as she struggled to gain control of her limbs. Her heart raced as the wind picked up, the howling gusts cutting through the air like a warning. The trees around her swayed unnaturally, bending in strange angles as though they were alive, their twisted branches reaching down toward her like skeletal hands.

Amara's breath hitched. She knew these woods. These were the same woods that bordered the village, the very same forest that had once felt like a place of comfort. But now? Now, it felt like a labyrinth, each shadow stretching farther, each gust of wind carrying a whisper that spoke her name.

"Amara."

The whisper was faint at first, so faint that she thought it was her imagination, or the wind playing tricks. But then it came again, stronger, insistent.

"Amara, you cannot escape."

She froze, her blood running cold. The voice—it was not her own. It was deeper, older, a sound that seemed to come from the very earth itself. Her stomach churned with a wave of nausea, and she tried to push back the fear clawing at her throat.

"Who's there?" she called out, her voice cracking, desperate. Her gaze darted between the trees, but there was no sign of movement, no figure stepping from the shadows. Yet she could feel it—something was out there, watching her.

"You are lost," the voice murmured, closer now, almost in her ear. Amara whipped around, her body rigid with terror, but the clearing was empty. Only the trees—those twisted, gnarled trees—stood as silent sentinels in the dark.

Her mind raced, scrambling for something to hold on to, something that could anchor her in this suffocating nightmare. The river—the river had always been a part of her life, a source of peace and comfort. But now, the thought of it made her blood run cold. Hadn't the ghost said the river had chosen her? And wasn't it the same force that had cursed her with this strange connection to the woman?

A cold, creeping realization began to settle in her gut—the river had always been more than just water. It was power. It was life, yes, but it was also death. And now, it was coming for her.

Her legs moved before she could stop them, instinct driving her forward. She had to get to the river. The only place where she could feel any semblance of clarity, the only place where she might understand what had happened to her.

The path through the woods seemed endless, each step dragging her deeper into the darkened heart of the forest. Her breath was ragged, her feet slipping on the damp earth as she pushed forward, her pulse hammering in her ears. She had no idea where she was going, only that she needed to find the river. She needed to find something—anything—that could explain this madness.

And then, she saw it.

Through the trees, faint at first but growing clearer with every step, the river appeared, winding through the woods like a dark, sinuous serpent. Its surface was as smooth as glass, reflecting the sickly glow of the moon that had finally broken through the clouds. The water looked calm, serene even, but Amara knew better. The river had never been calm. It had always been watching, waiting.

She reached the bank, her legs shaking with exhaustion. Her fingers tightened around the cool earth, grounding her, as she knelt at the edge of the river. She could hear it now—the murmur of the water, soft but relentless, as if it were speaking to her, beckoning her closer.

"Come to me, Amara," the voice whispered again, echoing in the river's song. *"You belong to me."*

She recoiled, her heart stuttering in her chest. This was it. This was the river's call—the pull she had been feeling all this time, like an invisible chain drawing her in.

But what did it want from her? Why her?

The ground beneath her trembled. At first, it was faint, but then the vibrations grew stronger, sending ripples through the water. Amara's breath caught in her throat as she stood, her gaze locked on the river's surface. It was no longer still. The water began to swirl and churn, twisting into shapes that made no sense, like a maelstrom being summoned from the depths.

Something was coming.

Suddenly, the water exploded outward, a massive wave rising from the center of the river, crashing against the bank with the force of a storm. Amara stumbled back, her heart racing.

And then, she saw it.

A figure rose from the water, towering and dark, its features obscured by the roiling currents. It was a shape, a shadow—a creature from the depths, a thing from the river that had come to claim her. It moved with unnatural grace, its form shifting and undulating, like water itself.

Amara froze, terror gripping her as the creature's gaze fixed on her. She could feel its eyes, though she couldn't see them. It was watching her, studying her.

You are the chosen one, the voice whispered once more, this time louder, clearer. It was coming from the creature. From the river itself. *You will join us. You will become one with the depths.*

Amara could hardly breathe. She stumbled backward, but her feet caught on the slick mud, sending her sprawling onto the ground. The creature was coming closer, its massive form slithering toward her, the water surrounding it parting like a sea. The darkness of the river was alive now, suffocating her, closing in around her like a net.

No, she thought, desperately fighting against the fear that was flooding her mind. *I won't be a part of this. I won't let it consume me.*

She scrambled to her feet, her heart hammering in her chest. The river's pull was stronger than ever, but she refused to let it take her. Not without understanding what it was—what it truly was.

But the darkness was too strong, the sky too heavy, the air too thick. As the creature approached, its form rising higher, Amara realized with a sickening certainty: this wasn't just the river. It was the power behind the river, the ancient force that had been watching her all along.

And now, it was here.

The sky above darkened further, as if the heavens themselves were preparing for the final reckoning. The wind howled again, and the river roared, its voice growing louder, more insistent.

Amara stood, rooted to the spot, knowing that there was no escape. Not anymore.

The darkening sky had come for her.

17

The Mark of the Past

Amara's breath came in shallow gasps as she stumbled away from the riverbank, the weight of the creature's presence pressing down on her chest. The air was thick, heavy with the scent of the earth and the iron tang of the water, but it felt like there was no air at all. Her heart beat too fast, her head spinning as she fought to stay grounded, to keep herself from being consumed by the dark forces she had uncovered.

The river, its surface still now, no longer roiling with the monstrous thing that had risen from its depths, seemed to mock her. It was as calm as it had always been—serene and beautiful, its waters reflecting the moonlight like a polished mirror. But she knew better now. She knew the river held more secrets than it had ever let on. Dark secrets that had been waiting for her all this time.

Amara's feet moved without thought, her legs carrying her forward, away from the pull of the water, away from the creature, away from the terror that had nearly swallowed her whole. The woods seemed to close in around her as she fled, the trees crowding together, their gnarled branches scraping against the sky like claws, the wind picking up in a frenzy.

But no matter how fast she moved, no matter how desperately she tried to outrun the suffocating darkness, she could still feel it. The weight of something unseen, pressing against her shoulders, urging her to turn back. To face what she had seen.

She had to understand. She had to know the truth.

Amara's mind screamed at her to stop, to rest, to breathe. But every time she tried to slow, her thoughts were drowned out by the sound of the river. The voice of the river.

"You are the chosen one, Amara."

Her hands shot to her ears as though she could block it out, but the whisper was inside her, inescapable, lodged deep within her mind, curling around her thoughts like a vine. The river wasn't just calling her—it was marking her.

You will join us. You will become one with the depths.

The words echoed in her mind with terrifying clarity. The river wasn't something distant or removed from her—it was inside her now, inside her veins, flowing through her blood. She could feel it, feel the connection, the mark it had left. It was as if a brand had been burned into her soul, an indelible sign that she belonged to something ancient, something vast and unknowable.

As she stumbled forward through the trees, her hand brushed against the rough bark of a nearby oak, the texture almost grounding her. The familiar feeling of the bark beneath her fingertips should have calmed her, should have brought her some sense of familiarity, but it did the opposite. The moment her skin touched the wood, a searing pain shot through her wrist, as though the tree itself had become a part of the curse that was chasing her.

Amara gasped, jerking her hand away. The pain lingered, throbbing in her veins, spreading from her wrist into her arm like wildfire. She glanced down, her stomach tightening with dread as she saw the mark. The skin around her wrist had darkened, a deep, blackened stain that had begun to spread across her palm, twisting in strange patterns that made no sense.

The mark of the past.

Her pulse quickened, her breath shallow and ragged. She didn't need to understand its meaning to know that it was something ancient, something tied to the river, to the forces that had claimed her. This was no ordinary wound. This wasn't just the pain from touching a tree—it was a sign, a marking of the curse that had been placed upon her.

"You are bound to us," the voice whispered again, this time with a finality that sent a chill down her spine. *"No matter how far you run, no matter how fast you flee, the mark will follow you. You will carry it for as long as you live."*

Amara closed her eyes, trying to block out the voice, trying to shut out the fear that threatened to consume her. She had always believed the river was a source of peace, of safety. But now, she understood—it was a force of nature, something older and far more powerful than she had ever realized. And it had chosen her.

She wasn't just a part of the village's history. She wasn't just tied to the river as an observer. The river had claimed her.

Tears welled in her eyes, but she refused to let them fall. She could not afford to break now, not when she was on the edge of something far darker than she had ever imagined. She had to fight. She had to survive.

She kept walking, the forest swallowing her with its shadowed embrace. The mark on her wrist burned like a brand, and every step she took felt heavier than the last. It was as if the earth itself was pulling her down, dragging her closer to whatever it was that lay ahead.

The path was familiar now. She had walked it many times before, but tonight it was different. The woods were oppressive, suffocating. The trees seemed to bend in on themselves, casting twisted shadows that danced in the flickering light of the moon. The wind howled in her ears, and yet the air was still. The only sound that reached her ears was the rhythmic pounding of her heartbeat, like a drum, urging her forward.

Then, just as she was about to collapse, she saw it.

Through the thick trees, there was a flicker of light. At first, she thought it was another illusion, the product of her racing thoughts and the terror that gripped her. But then, as she drew closer, she saw it more clearly. A fire.

A fire burning in the center of a clearing.

Amara's breath caught in her throat as she realized where she was. This was the place. The place where she had been taken as a child, the clearing that had been so familiar to her, the place where the elders had performed their rituals—before she had understood what they truly meant.

And now, the fire burned brighter, casting long, eerie shadows on the trees surrounding the clearing.

Her feet carried her forward, though her mind screamed for her to turn back. She had to see it. She had to understand what this place had to do with the mark, with the river, with the thing inside her that was growing stronger by the minute.

As she approached the fire, she saw them—figures standing in a circle around the flames. They were dressed in long, dark robes, their faces hidden by hoods. They didn't move, but she could feel their gaze on her, as if they were waiting for her to arrive.

Amara's breath caught in her throat as she stepped closer. She had seen this before, but she hadn't understood it. The rituals, the fire, the chanting—it was all connected. These people—these figures—were part of the same force that had marked her. They were the keepers, the watchers, the ones who had called the river's power into the world.

And they were waiting for her.

The mark on her wrist throbbed with painful intensity, as though it recognized them, as though it was drawing her closer to them.

You are mine, the voice whispered one last time, louder now, more insistent than ever. *And you will fulfill your destiny.*

Amara's body went cold as she realized the truth.

The fire was not just a symbol of power.

It was a signal. A summoning.

And she had come to answer it.

18

The Forbidden Kiss

The fire blazed ahead of her, the flames dancing with an intensity that seemed unnatural, crackling and hissing as though the wood itself was resisting its fate. The heat from the fire prickled Amara's skin, but it wasn't enough to chase away the cold that had settled in her bones. Her eyes were drawn to the figures encircling the fire—those robed figures, standing motionless as if they were part of the night itself. Their faces remained hidden, their bodies casting long, foreboding shadows across the ground, merging with the darkness in a way that made it impossible to discern where they ended and the forest began.

Amara's heart pounded louder in her ears as she stepped forward, though every inch of her body screamed for her to turn back. The mark on her wrist was burning now, a fire that came from within, as though the river itself had woven its essence into her very flesh. Her breaths came shallow, the air around her thick with anticipation, like a living thing, wrapping itself around her chest.

The moment her foot crossed into the clearing, the wind seemed to die, leaving only the crackling of the fire and the distant call of the night creatures. She looked at the figures, her throat tight with dread. But it wasn't just their presence that unsettled her—it was the feeling that they had been expecting her. That they had been waiting for this moment for longer than she had known.

One of the figures moved, just a slight shift, but it was enough to draw her attention. The robes fluttered, revealing the slightest hint of a silhouette, a shape she couldn't quite place. Then the figure stepped forward, the others shifting aside like shadows to allow him to approach her.

A chill ran through Amara as the man—tall, his face hidden beneath the hood—stopped before her. She could feel his gaze, cold and piercing, even though she couldn't see his eyes. The air around them seemed to thrum with an energy that she couldn't understand, something ancient and powerful that had been stirred by her presence.

"Amara," his voice was like a whisper, but it cut through the silence with a clarity that made her heart stutter. "You have come."

Her body tensed as the man reached out, his fingers brushing against her wrist, where the mark still pulsed with fiery intensity. The touch was cold, like the depths of the river, but it sent a wave of heat through her, pooling in the pit of her stomach. She flinched, but his hand didn't pull away.

"Why?" she whispered, her voice barely audible above the crackling flames. "What is this? What do you want from me?"

He tilted his head slightly, as if considering her question, then looked down at her wrist. His fingers tightened, and Amara's pulse quickened. She knew he could feel it—the mark, the connection. The bond that was now a part of her, a bond that tied her to him, to the river, and to whatever this ritual had become.

"You were always meant to come," he said, his voice a soft murmur that sent a shiver down her spine. "The river chose you. And now, the time has come to complete what was started."

Before she could respond, he stepped closer, his robes brushing against her. Her body instinctively moved back, but he caught her wrist, his grip firm and unyielding.

"Do not fight it," he said, his voice almost tender now, as if trying to soothe her fear. But it only made the unease in her chest deepen. "You will come to understand soon enough. All things are connected, Amara. The river, the fire, the land—"

His words were cut off by a sudden pull of energy, something that seemed to draw her toward him against her will. The air crackled with electricity, a force too strong to resist. Her chest tightened as if she couldn't breathe. The mark on her wrist flared to life, the dark veins of it pulsing in rhythm with the fire. And then, before she could stop herself, her lips parted in a breathless gasp, and the man's mouth descended upon hers.

It was not a kiss born of love, nor of desire, but of something much darker, much deeper. His lips were cold, like the river's depths, but they seared her skin as though they were burning her from the inside out. His kiss was all-consuming—utterly possessive—and she felt the world around her collapse into the sensation of his touch. It was as though he was pulling her apart, piece by piece, unraveling her in ways she didn't know were possible.

Every breath she took seemed to be stolen from her, every thought she had scattered into oblivion. There was nothing but him, his coldness, his power. The mark on her wrist burned so fiercely now that she thought it might consume her entirely.

But then, just as suddenly as it had begun, the kiss broke. Amara gasped, stumbling back as if waking from a dream—no, from a nightmare. Her body shook, the lingering heat of his touch still scorching her lips, her skin, and something deep inside her soul.

The man stepped back, his expression unreadable beneath the hood. His hand dropped to his side, but the weight of his touch still lingered, like an invisible chain that kept her tethered to him.

For a long moment, neither of them spoke. The fire crackled and roared, but it felt distant now, as if the world outside of this clearing had faded into irrelevance.

Amara's breath was shallow, her chest heaving as she tried to process what had just happened. The kiss—the forbidden kiss—had been more than just an exchange of lips. It had been a sealing, an irreversible act that bound her to him, to the river, to this ancient force she had only begun to understand.

"What... what did you do to me?" Her voice was raw, trembling with the weight of the question, the terror in her chest.

The man remained silent for a long moment, the flames reflecting in his eyes, though she couldn't see his face clearly. Then, his voice came again, low and cold.

"I did nothing," he said, his words echoing in the stillness. "It was always meant to be this way. The kiss was the final step. The mark has been placed, and now, you will begin to understand."

The realization hit her like a cold gust of wind. The kiss had been more than a ritual. It had been the completion of something that had been set in motion long before she ever entered the woods. The mark, the connection to the river, the bond she had felt with the water—it had all led to this.

"You belong to the river now," the man said, his voice almost gentle, like a whisper of wind through the trees. "And the river will have its due."

The words sent a cold shiver through Amara's veins. She was no longer just a part of the village's story. She was no longer just a girl who had once felt the river's pull.

She was its vessel now.

As the man turned to rejoin the circle of figures, Amara's mind reeled. The kiss, the mark, the river—it was all happening too fast, too suddenly. But there was no turning back now. The river had claimed her, and in doing so, it had marked her forever.

And now, she would have to face what that truly meant.

19

The Betrayal

The air had grown thick with tension, heavy and suffocating, as Amara stood at the edge of the clearing. The fire had dwindled to little more than a smoldering heap of embers, casting long shadows that seemed to stretch like fingers into the dark forest. The figures had gone, their presence now just a lingering chill in the air. The eerie stillness of the night pressed down on her chest, and the mark on her wrist—still burning from the kiss—throbbed with a rhythm of its own, as though it had a life separate from hers.

Amara's thoughts were a jumbled mess, swirling around her like the smoke from the fire, and she couldn't quite make sense of any of it. The kiss, the ritual, the river—it was all too much. Too much for a girl like her, a girl who had once believed in the simplicity of her life in the village. A girl who had thought that the biggest mystery was the old tales her mother used to tell by the fire.

But now, those stories were no longer just stories. They were her reality. And the truth—whatever it was—was slipping through her fingers like sand.

Her legs trembled, and she could feel the weight of the night pressing against her, the promise of something much darker looming over her every step. It was then that she heard it—a rustle of leaves, a soft step on the dirt path behind her. She spun around, her heart leaping in her chest, but the person who stood before her was not the man from the circle. It was someone much more familiar.

"Amara," Kofi's voice was strained, but he was trying to sound calm, trying to soothe her. His eyes were wide, his gaze flicking nervously to the woods around them. "I've been looking for you. I was afraid—"

Amara didn't let him finish. "Why didn't you warn me, Kofi?" Her voice cracked as she spoke, and she hated the way it sounded—vulnerable, desperate. "Why didn't you tell me what they were planning? What I was about to become?"

Kofi took a step forward, his face twisting with guilt. "I didn't—"

"Don't lie!" Amara shouted, the anger rising in her throat like bile. Her fingers tightened around her wrist, feeling the burning mark pulse against her skin as if to remind her of the curse she had been drawn into. "You knew. You knew what was happening, and you said nothing. You stood there, watched me—" She stopped herself, the weight of the truth settling over her like a shadow.

Kofi's expression faltered, his lips parted as though he were trying to say something, but no words came out. Instead, he just stood there, his eyes filled with something unreadable. Guilt? Fear? Or something darker? It was impossible for Amara to tell.

"I didn't know how to protect you," Kofi murmured finally, his voice tight, strained with emotion. "I didn't know what to do. They said you would be chosen, that it was part of the plan. I didn't want to believe it. I didn't want to see you get hurt."

Amara's hands were trembling now, her body shaking with the intensity of the emotions swirling inside her. Her eyes narrowed as she took a step back, her gaze never leaving Kofi's face. The pieces of the puzzle were falling into place, but none of them fit the way she wanted them to. "So you knew I was going to become part of this ritual, but you just let me go? You let them do this to me?"

"No," Kofi said quickly, his voice rising. "I never wanted this. I swear it. I only wanted to protect you. But the elders, Amara... they said it was fate. They said it was written in the stars, that the river had chosen you. I couldn't stop it. I couldn't stop them."

Amara's throat tightened, a sharp pang of betrayal piercing her chest. She had always trusted Kofi. He had been her friend, her confidant. And now, she realized, he had been standing by, watching, while the very thing she had feared most happened to her.

"You should have fought for me," she whispered, the weight of her words cutting through the air like a blade. "You should have stopped it. You should have warned me, Kofi. Instead, you just stood there. You—"

Kofi flinched as if her words were physical blows. "I couldn't, Amara. I couldn't. If I had spoken out... if I had tried to stop them, they would have done something worse. The river is powerful, more powerful than anything I could have imagined. It doesn't just choose anyone. It chooses those it needs."

Her eyes widened in realization, the truth crashing down on her like a tidal wave. Kofi wasn't just afraid for her—he was afraid of them. Of the elders. Of the river. And, in a way, he had been protecting her by staying silent, by letting the events unfold without interference. But what kind of protection was that?

"What are you saying, Kofi?" she asked, her voice low and dangerous now. The anger that had been simmering beneath the surface was boiling over, consuming her from the inside. "That you let this happen to me because you were afraid? You were too afraid to fight for me?"

Kofi's eyes hardened, his shoulders stiffening as he took a step back. "I'm not afraid of you, Amara," he said, his voice suddenly cold, his gaze narrowing as if to shut her out. "But I am afraid of what the river can do. What it will do if it doesn't get what it wants."

A silence fell between them, a heavy, suffocating silence that seemed to stretch on for an eternity. Amara could feel her pulse in her throat, pounding against her skin, her heart hammering with rage and confusion. Kofi had just admitted something—something dark, something she couldn't ignore. He wasn't just afraid of the river. He had chosen to stand by while it took her.

And, in that moment, she understood.

It wasn't just the elders who had betrayed her. It was Kofi, too. The boy she had trusted, the boy who had promised to protect her. He had known what was coming. He had known the danger she was walking into. And he had done nothing.

"All this time," she said, her voice trembling with a mix of disbelief and hurt, "I thought you cared about me. I thought you wanted to help me. But you're just like them, aren't you? You're just like all of them."

Kofi's face twisted, a flash of pain crossing his features before it was quickly replaced with a wall of cold indifference. "I never wanted this for you, Amara," he said, the words coming out like ice. "But there's no stopping it now. You've already been marked. You're already part of it."

Amara stepped back, the betrayal cutting deeper than anything she had ever felt. Her hands clenched at her sides, the mark on her wrist flaring in response, the heat of it burning like fire through her skin.

"You were the one person I thought I could trust," she said, her voice barely more than a whisper. "But I was wrong."

And as she turned to leave, the sound of her footsteps crunching on the dirt was the only thing that followed her, a grim reminder of the fractured trust between them.

In the distance, the river called, its dark, endless pull beckoning her. And with it, the promise of something far worse than betrayal—something that would change her forever.

20

The Coming Storm

The night had fallen heavy and oppressive, the weight of it sinking into Amara's bones, pulling her deeper into the forest, away from the village and the betrayal that had broken her heart. Kofi's words still echoed in her mind, though she tried to silence them. **"You're already part of it."** The mark on her wrist burned, a constant reminder of the river's claim, of the ancient force that now tethered her to something far darker than anything she had ever imagined.

She walked in silence, the only sound the crunch of leaves beneath her feet and the occasional rustle of branches swaying in the wind. The forest seemed alive around her, as though the trees were whispering secrets she could not understand. The moonlight filtered through the canopy above, casting eerie shadows that twisted and writhed like dark figures watching her every move.

Amara's heart pounded, a drumbeat of fear and anger. She had trusted Kofi—trusted him with her heart, with her dreams, with her very life. But now... now she saw the truth. He had never been on her side. He had stood by while the river claimed her, while the ritual unfolded with its insidious purpose. **He had let it happen.**

Her hands clenched into fists at her sides, her nails digging into her palms as she fought back the rising tide of fury. **I won't let them use me.** The thought was a mantra now, something that steeled her resolve as she pushed forward, deeper into the heart of the forest. There was something she had to find—something she had to do before it was too late.

And then she heard it.

At first, it was nothing more than a faint rumble, like distant thunder, but it grew louder, until the ground beneath her feet seemed to tremble with the intensity of it. The air had grown heavy, thick with the scent of rain and the electricity of an approaching storm. Amara stopped in her tracks, her breath hitching in her throat. **This isn't natural.**

Her eyes scanned the darkness around her, searching for the source of the disturbance, but all she saw were the trees, their silhouettes swaying in the wind. The rumble grew louder still, and now she could hear the unmistakable sound of rushing water. The river.

It was moving. The river was calling to her, and not in the way it had before. This was different. This was urgent, angry. The ground beneath her feet began to quake, and she stumbled forward, caught off guard by the intensity of the vibration. She heard the crack of branches snapping and the distant crash of trees falling. The forest was alive with a terrifying energy, as if the earth itself was being torn apart.

I have to get to the river.

Amara broke into a run, her heart hammering in her chest as the world around her seemed to twist and collapse under the weight of the storm. The wind howled in her ears, pulling at her clothes, and the trees groaned as though they, too, were being dragged into the fury of whatever force had been awakened. The sound of rushing water grew louder, louder still, until it drowned out everything else—the wind, the trees, even the beating of her own heart.

As she neared the riverbank, the sight that greeted her stopped her in her tracks.

The river was swollen, its waters churning violently, rising higher than she had ever seen them. The dark water roiled like a beast in pain, pulling at the banks as though it were alive, desperate to escape its confines. The wind whipped the surface of the river, sending spray into the air like sheets of cold rain. The air around the river felt charged, as though the very atmosphere were on the brink of collapse.

Amara's breath came in ragged gasps as she stepped closer to the edge, her eyes fixed on the dark, swirling waters. The mark on her wrist burned hotter than ever, and she could feel the pull—the river was calling to her, its voice no longer a soft whisper, but a roar in her ears, demanding that she join it.

Suddenly, a figure appeared from the shadows. At first, Amara thought it was just another trick of the wind, but then the figure stepped closer, and she saw him clearly. It was the man from the ritual—the one who had kissed her, who had marked her with the river's curse. His hood was pulled back now, revealing his face. His eyes glowed with an unnatural light, the color of storm clouds on the horizon. His lips curled into a smile, one that was as cold as the water that churned at his feet.

"You've come," he said, his voice deep and resonant, like the rumble of thunder. "I knew you would."

Amara took a step back, her heart racing. "What is happening?" she demanded, her voice trembling. "Why is the river like this? What do you want from me?"

The man's smile widened. "It's not what I want, Amara. It's what the river wants. It has been waiting for you, for the chosen one. And now, the storm is here. The river's fury is coming. And you—" he paused, his gaze locking with hers, "—you will be its conduit."

Amara's blood ran cold. "Conduit? What do you mean?"

"The storm is the river's reckoning," he said, his voice low and hypnotic. "The balance has been disturbed. The forces that have held the river at bay are weakening. And you... you are the key. You are the one who will bring the river's power to fruition."

The ground beneath her feet rumbled again, more violently this time, as if the earth itself were protesting. The river's roar grew louder, and the air seemed to crackle with the intensity of the storm that was rapidly approaching. The figure moved closer, his presence suffocating in the charged atmosphere.

"It is too late to turn back now, Amara," he said, his voice almost a whisper, though it carried across the roaring wind. "You have been marked. You are the river's chosen. The storm will come, and with it, the power of the river will rise. And you… you will be its vessel."

Amara shook her head, her mind a whirlwind of thoughts and fear. This wasn't just about the river anymore. This wasn't just about the ritual or the kiss. This was something much worse. The storm was not merely a natural disaster—it was the manifestation of the river's wrath, its desire to reclaim what had been taken from it. And she was the one who had been chosen to carry out its will.

"No!" Amara cried out, taking a step back, but the man reached out, grabbing her wrist with surprising force. The mark flared to life again, burning hot against her skin, and she gasped in pain.

"You have no choice," he said, his voice colder now, more insistent. "The storm is coming, Amara. The river is rising, and you are its vessel. Whether you accept it or not, the power will consume you. It's already begun."

Amara's heart pounded in her chest as she looked into his glowing eyes, fear pooling in her stomach like ice. The storm was not just coming. It had already arrived. And she was at the center of it.

As the wind howled louder and the earth trembled beneath her feet, Amara realized, with a sinking feeling in her chest, that this was no longer a battle for survival. This was the beginning of something far darker.

And she had no idea if she was strong enough to stop it.

21

The Echoes of History

The storm had raged through the night, relentless and wild, but as dawn began to break, it left the world in a strange, uneasy stillness. The wind had died down, but the air was thick, heavy with the scent of rain and the promise of something more. The sky, though clearing, remained an ominous shade of dark gray, the clouds still swirling above like the remnants of an ancient storm that refused to let go.

Amara stood at the edge of the riverbank, her eyes fixed on the waters, now calmer, but still churning with an unnatural energy beneath the surface. The mark on her wrist burned with every passing moment, each pulse reminding her that she was tethered to something far greater, far darker, than anything she had ever imagined. The figure—the man who had revealed the truth to her—had disappeared as quickly as he had come, leaving her standing alone in the aftermath of his words.

"You are the river's vessel. The storm is your legacy."

The words echoed in her mind like a haunting refrain. How could she, a simple girl from the village, be the key to something so ancient, so powerful? The river had chosen her, yes. But why? Why her? What made her special enough to bear such a burden?

The rustling of leaves pulled her from her thoughts. She turned sharply, her pulse quickening, her instincts on edge. Out of the shadows of the trees, a figure emerged—one she hadn't expected. It was Kofi.

He looked different. There was a hardness to his expression now, a coldness that hadn't been there before. His clothes were soaked from the storm, his hair damp and matted against his forehead, but it wasn't the rain that made him seem distant—it was the look in his eyes. His usual warmth was gone, replaced with an unreadable emptiness.

Amara's heart sank as he approached, his steps slow, deliberate. For a moment, neither of them spoke. The silence between them was thick, suffocating, as if the weight of everything that had happened was pressing down on them both.

"You left," Amara finally said, her voice sharp. "You left me there—alone. After everything. You just walked away."

Kofi stopped a few feet from her, his gaze not meeting hers. "I didn't have a choice, Amara."

Her chest tightened at the words. "You always had a choice, Kofi. You just didn't care enough to make the right one."

Kofi flinched, but he didn't deny it. Instead, he exhaled sharply, as if he had been holding his breath for far too long. "I'm not the one who decided this. I never wanted you to be part of the river. I never wanted you to be caught in this... this mess."

"Then why didn't you stop it?" she demanded, her voice rising with the frustration that had been building within her since the ritual. "Why didn't you tell me what they were planning? Why did you let them take me, let them mark me? You could have protected me, Kofi."

He finally looked up at her, his eyes dark, haunted. "I tried. You don't understand. I tried to warn you, but they're too powerful. The elders, the river... they're all connected, bound by forces that are beyond us. I couldn't fight them. I didn't want to see you hurt, but..." His voice faltered. "You were always going to be part of this. It's written in the history of our people. The river calls, and it doesn't let go."

Amara felt a chill run through her. "History? What are you talking about?"

Kofi's gaze turned distant, and for a long moment, he said nothing. When he finally spoke again, his voice was low, almost a whisper, as if the very words were too heavy to bear.

"Do you remember the stories?" he asked, his eyes narrowing as though searching her face for something. "The old tales our people tell?

The stories of the river gods, the rituals, the sacrifices made to keep the balance... They're not just stories, Amara. They're our history."

Amara's breath caught in her throat. She knew the stories, of course. Everyone did. The legends of the river that ran through the heart of their village, the river that had always been both a source of life and a force of destruction. The elders had spoken of the river's power, its hunger, but they had always been vague, as though the full truth was too dangerous to speak aloud.

But now, in the stillness of the storm's aftermath, Kofi's words hit her like a thunderclap.

"The river has always chosen a vessel," he continued, his voice thick with sorrow. "Every few generations, a child is born with a connection to it—a connection that can never be severed. The river needs someone to carry its power, to channel its will. And you... you're the one it chose this time. You were always meant to be its vessel."

Amara felt her world tilt. "But why me?" she whispered, the question tearing at her chest. "I didn't ask for this. I didn't choose this."

"You don't choose the river," Kofi said softly, his voice full of an ancient sorrow that she couldn't comprehend. "It chooses you. It chooses those who are connected to the very blood of the earth, to the spirit of the river itself. It's in your lineage, Amara. Your mother... your grandmother... they were part of this too."

Amara staggered backward, her mind reeling. "What do you mean? My mother never said anything—"

Kofi shook his head, cutting her off. "Your mother didn't know. She didn't want to know. But the elders... they've always known. Your bloodline has always been tied to the river's power, and now, it's your turn to bear the burden. There's no escaping it."

The words hung in the air, heavy and suffocating, and Amara could feel the ground beneath her feet shift. Her mind spun, trying to grasp what he was telling her. **Her bloodline. Her mother.** It was too much—too much to take in all at once.

"Why didn't you tell me this before?" she asked, her voice trembling with both anger and disbelief. "Why wait until now?"

Kofi's eyes darkened with shame. "I didn't want you to be afraid. I didn't want you to see the truth, because the truth means that you are bound to the river now. It means that the storm is coming, and you have no choice but to face it."

Amara closed her eyes, trying to block out the flood of emotions rushing through her. The weight of history, of her ancestors, pressing down on her with an unbearable force. She had thought she was just a girl caught up in something she didn't understand, but now, she realized, she was part of something much bigger—something that had been set in motion long before she was born.

"The storm," she whispered, her heart sinking as the realization hit her like a tidal wave. "It's not just the weather. It's the river's wrath."

Kofi nodded grimly. "The river is waking up, Amara. The balance is broken, and the storm is just the beginning. The power that the river holds—it's not just for our people anymore. It wants more. And you, you are its chosen vessel."

A shudder ran through her as the enormity of his words settled in her chest like ice. **The coming storm**—it was a storm of history, of power, of blood. And she was at the center of it, trapped between the past and a future she couldn't escape.

The echoes of history were louder now, pounding in her ears, and she realized, with a sinking feeling, that there was no turning back. She was tied to the river. And soon, she would have to face what it truly meant to be its chosen one.

The storm was coming. And nothing would ever be the same again.

22

The Shattered Promise

Amara stood at the edge of the river, her breath shallow, her heart a drumbeat that echoed in her chest. The waters before her were calm now, a deceptive tranquility that masked the storm lurking beneath the surface. She could feel it, deep in her bones—something was shifting, something ancient and powerful, and it was all converging upon her. She had once believed that the river had chosen her, but now she understood the truth: she had never been given a choice. The river had marked her, bound her to its will, and it would never let her go.

Kofi's words rang in her ears like a warning she could not escape. **"The storm is just the beginning."**

She looked out across the river, her thoughts a tangled mess. She should have been angry—she should have screamed, shouted at him for the betrayal, for the lies he had fed her. But all she could do was stand there, helpless, as the promise she had made to herself—**the promise to fight for her freedom, for her choice**—seemed to slip further and further away, like sand through her fingers.

"Amara?"

She jumped, startled by the sound of her name breaking the silence. Turning sharply, she saw him. **Kofi.**

His figure appeared out of the mist, as though he had risen from the very river itself, a haunting presence against the pale light of the morning. His hair, still damp from the storm, clung to his forehead, and his eyes were shadowed, hollow with regret. But there was something else, something darker that made Amara's blood run cold.

His gaze met hers, and for a moment, neither of them moved. The world felt suspended in that instant, as though time itself had paused to let them understand the magnitude of what was happening between them.

"What do you want, Kofi?" Her voice was strained, edged with a quiet fury she hadn't known she was capable of. She knew what he would say, but it didn't stop the question from spilling out.

"I want to make things right," Kofi said, his voice low, as though he were afraid of the words themselves.

"Make things right?" She let out a bitter laugh, her gaze turning back to the river, as if the dark waters would offer some comfort. "You've already destroyed everything. What's left to fix?"

Kofi took a hesitant step toward her, and she could see the conflict in his eyes. The same conflict that had been there since the beginning—the hesitation that had stopped him from warning her, from protecting her. The hesitation that had allowed the ritual to unfold, that had allowed the river to claim her.

"I never wanted this for you," he whispered, his voice breaking the stillness around them. "I swear to you, Amara. I never wanted you to be a part of this. But the elders... they made the decision long before you or I were born. The river has always called for someone. And now it's your turn. You don't have a choice."

"I didn't ask for your protection!" She flung the words at him, her chest tight with fury. "You didn't protect me, Kofi. You abandoned me. You let them do this to me, to us!"

Kofi's eyes were full of remorse, his jaw clenched as though fighting against the rising tide of emotion threatening to overwhelm him. He took another step closer, and this time, Amara didn't step back. "I couldn't stop it," he said, his voice barely audible. "You think I didn't want to? I tried. I tried to tell you everything, to warn you, but the elders—they would have killed me if I interfered. The river's will is too strong. The storm is coming, Amara. There's nothing we can do to stop it."

Her breath caught in her throat at the finality of his words. She wanted to scream at him, to tell him that it wasn't his decision to make, that he had no right to speak for her. But all that came out was a broken, disbelieving laugh.

"Then why did you make me promise?" Amara's voice trembled with the weight of the question. "Why did you make me believe I had a choice in all of this?"

Kofi's face softened, his eyes pleading with her, as if there were still a part of him that thought he could fix this, that he could undo the damage done. But Amara could see the truth in his eyes now—the same truth that had been hidden behind his promises, his warm smiles, his carefully crafted words.

"You didn't understand," he said, his voice thick with regret. "I wanted to protect you, Amara. I swore to myself that I would protect you, no matter the cost. But now... now I see that I've only made things worse."

Amara shook her head, her heart twisting in her chest. She wanted to believe him, she really did. But the pain of his betrayal, the weight of the shattered promise that had bound them, was too much to ignore.

"The storm," she whispered, more to herself than to him. "It's coming, and there's nothing we can do to stop it, is there?"

Kofi's eyes darkened, and for the first time, Amara saw the true weight of what they were facing reflected in his gaze. "No," he said quietly. "There's nothing we can do. The storm will come, and the river's will will be carried out. Whether we want it or not."

The words hung between them like a death sentence. Amara closed her eyes, fighting back the tears that threatened to spill. She had promised herself that she would never become a vessel for the river's wrath. She had promised herself that she would fight, that she would break free from this fate. But now, standing on the precipice of the storm, she knew that the promise she had made to herself was already broken. The river had won.

And so had Kofi.

Her heart shattered in that moment, not just for the loss of her own freedom, but for the loss of everything she had believed in. The promise they had shared, the trust they had built—everything was gone. It was as if the river had claimed it all, swallowed it whole, leaving nothing but emptiness in its wake.

"You should go," Amara said, her voice barely above a whisper. "There's nothing left for us here."

Kofi stood frozen, his face a mask of pain and regret. "Amara..."

"Go," she repeated, her voice harder now, a final plea for him to leave her in peace. "Please."

For a long moment, neither of them moved. Then, slowly, Kofi turned away, his shoulders slumped, as if the weight of the decision had crushed him. Amara watched him go, her heart breaking with each step he took away from her.

As he disappeared into the shadows of the trees, Amara's knees buckled, and she collapsed onto the cold earth. Her hand instinctively went to the mark on her wrist, the brand of the river that had sealed her fate.

She had been betrayed. She had been used.

And now, all that was left was the coming storm—the storm she could not escape.

The promise was shattered. And there was no turning back.

23

The Winter Garden

The cold air bit at Amara's skin as she walked through the dense thicket of trees, the path barely visible under the weight of a thick, wet fog that seemed to hang in the air like a shroud. The morning was still, the silence broken only by the faint rustle of leaves as the wind swept through the branches above. But even the wind felt wrong today—frigid and unsettling, as if nature itself was holding its breath.

Amara's footsteps were slow and deliberate, her mind still heavy with the weight of Kofi's betrayal. She couldn't shake the image of his face, the way he had looked at her with such sorrow in his eyes, as though he had lost something too. She could almost hear his voice in her mind again, the words he had spoken like daggers in her chest.

"The storm is coming. There's nothing we can do to stop it."

But there had to be something. There had to be a way out. Amara refused to believe that the river's will, or Kofi's guilt, had sealed her fate. She wouldn't let them. Not after everything she had fought for, not after everything that had been taken from her. The promise she had made to herself—to never let the river control her—still burned in her chest. She had to find a way to break free, to stop the coming storm before it was too late.

As she trudged through the mist, her eyes caught sight of something through the trees—a flicker of color in the distance, a patch of vibrant green standing out against the dreary landscape. Amara's heart skipped a beat. She knew this place. **The Winter Garden.**

It was a place of legend, whispered about in hushed voices by the elders when they thought no one was listening. It was said to be a garden hidden deep within the forest, where the coldest winters could never touch the plants that bloomed there. Flowers that never withered, fruits that never spoiled. It was a place of impossible beauty, untouched by the ravages of time, and it was said to hold secrets—secrets that could change everything.

She hadn't seen it herself, not in all her years in the village, but she had heard the stories. And now, standing on the threshold of that forgotten place, she felt an inexplicable pull, as though the garden itself was calling her, beckoning her to enter.

Without thinking, she stepped forward, her feet light against the damp ground as she moved closer to the mysterious garden. The trees parted just enough for her to slip through, and as she did, she was immediately struck by the stark contrast between the dark woods and the ethereal beauty of the garden before her.

It was more magnificent than she had imagined. The garden stretched out in every direction, its borders defined not by walls or fences, but by a natural barrier of overgrown vines and twisted trees. The flowers were unlike any Amara had ever seen—deep purples, fiery oranges, and delicate blues, all glowing faintly in the dim light as if they were alive with some kind of hidden magic. The scent of jasmine and something sweeter filled the air, mingling with the coldness that had followed her from the outside world.

But what struck her most was the silence. The silence that felt almost oppressive, as though the garden was holding its breath, waiting for something—or someone.

Her heart raced as she stepped deeper into the garden, her feet crunching softly on the frost-covered earth. As she moved, her eyes were drawn to the center of the garden, where an ancient stone pedestal stood, covered in moss and ivy. On it rested a single object, a small, delicate vial filled with a shimmering liquid that seemed to pulse with an otherworldly light.

Amara approached the pedestal slowly, drawn to the vial like a moth to a flame. She reached out, her fingers trembling as she picked it up, the glass cold against her skin. The liquid inside sparkled with an intensity that made her pulse quicken.

The moment her fingers closed around it, the ground beneath her feet seemed to shift. The air around her grew heavier, the silence thickening until it felt like the world itself was holding its breath. Amara's heart pounded in her chest as she turned the vial over in her hands. What was it? What power did it hold?

Suddenly, she felt a presence behind her, an unmistakable sense of being watched. She spun around, her pulse racing, her breath catching in her throat. Standing at the edge of the garden was a figure—a silhouette bathed in the faint glow of the flowers.

Amara's heart stilled. **The figure was Kofi.**

"Why are you here?" she demanded, her voice sharp with a mixture of anger and confusion. The vial in her hand felt heavier now, as if the very act of holding it had summoned him back into her world. "What do you want from me?"

Kofi's expression was unreadable, his face obscured by the shadows of the trees. "You shouldn't have come here," he said quietly, his voice low, almost reverent. "This place... it's not meant for you."

Amara felt a chill wash over her. "Not meant for me?" she repeated, her grip tightening on the vial. "Why not? What is this place?"

Kofi took a hesitant step forward, his eyes flickering to the vial in her hand before meeting her gaze. "The Winter Garden," he whispered, as though the name itself carried a weight of something forbidden. "It holds the answers you've been looking for. But it also holds the price. Every secret comes with a cost, Amara."

Amara felt a shiver run down her spine as she looked around, her gaze sweeping over the garden once more. The flowers seemed to shimmer in the dim light, their petals almost glowing with an otherworldly radiance. But the beauty of it all only deepened her unease. Something wasn't right. Kofi's presence here was not a coincidence.

"What price?" she asked, her voice low and guarded. She wasn't sure if she wanted to know, but she could feel the weight of it in her chest, heavy and unrelenting.

Kofi's eyes darkened, and for a brief moment, his vulnerability slipped through, his carefully constructed walls crumbling. "The price is the same as always. To learn the truth, you must give something up. A part of yourself."

Amara's breath hitched, her mind racing. "What part of myself?"

Kofi hesitated, as though struggling with the words. "The river... it is more than just a force of nature. It is a living thing, a spirit that has existed long before our people. The Winter Garden holds the key to understanding it. But it is not without sacrifice. If you wish to stop the storm—if you want to break the river's hold over you—you must give it something in return."

Amara felt the weight of his words settle deep within her, a suffocating presence that threatened to swallow her whole. "What are you asking me to do?"

Kofi stepped closer, his voice barely above a whisper. "You must choose, Amara. The river will not let you go unless you take its power. But to do that, you will have to become something else. Something... more."

Amara felt the air around her crackle with energy. The vial in her hand pulsed with an unnatural force, as though it were alive. Her heart raced as she stared at Kofi, trying to make sense of everything he was telling her. **The river's power. The storm. The price.**

Her gaze shifted back to the garden, to the flowers that seemed to hold the answers she sought. But as she looked at them, a thought lodged itself deep within her mind. **What was she willing to sacrifice?**

The silence grew, thick and heavy, until it was unbearable. She could feel the weight of Kofi's eyes on her, the intensity of his presence urging her toward something she wasn't sure she was ready for.

The Winter Garden had offered her a glimpse of the answers. But what would she have to lose in order to claim them?

The price was steep. But the storm was coming. And Amara knew she had little time left to decide.

24

The Heart's Choice

The air felt suffocating as Amara stood in the heart of the Winter Garden, the weight of Kofi's words lingering like a heavy fog. The vial in her hand pulsed with an energy she could barely comprehend, and the garden around her seemed to bend and shift, the flowers glowing eerily in the dim light. The world felt suspended, as if time had stopped, holding its breath for the decision she was about to make.

Kofi stood just a few feet away, his gaze fixed on her, his eyes shadowed with an emotion she couldn't quite name. He had always been a presence in her life, a constant—yet now, in the midst of this impossible choice, he felt more like a stranger than ever before. The very air between them seemed thick with unspoken words, as if neither of them dared to break the silence that had settled in the space.

Amara's heart raced. Her mind screamed at her to think, to make the right choice. But what was the right choice? How could she possibly know? The storm was coming, that much was certain, and the river was already pulling at her, trying to drag her into its depths. She could feel it, the power surging within her, tugging at her soul like an invisible thread. The promise Kofi had made to her, the promise of protection, had unraveled, leaving only raw truth in its wake. The river had chosen her, whether she wanted it or not.

But now, standing at the crossroads, the real question was this: Could she make the river her own? Could she harness its power, wield it to stop the storm, and in doing so, destroy the very force that had haunted her for so long?

The thought was both tempting and terrifying.

Kofi stepped closer, his voice low and cautious. "Amara, please. You don't understand what you're about to do. The river, the Winter Garden—it's not just a path to power. It's a curse. You'll become something else. Something... not entirely human."

She swallowed hard, her throat dry. The vial in her hand seemed to grow heavier with every passing second, the liquid inside shimmering with an almost hypnotic glow. Her fingers trembled, and for a moment, she wondered if it was fear or something else entirely—something darker—coursing through her veins. Her gaze flickered back to Kofi, who was watching her with a mixture of fear and sorrow.

He wasn't wrong. She had heard the stories—the ones whispered in hushed tones around the village fires, the ones about those who had tried to take the river's power for themselves. They had all been consumed. The elders said the price was always too high, that no one could ever truly control the river without losing themselves in the process.

Amara's breath hitched as she thought of the storm—the storm that was coming, that was already spreading its tendrils across the land, threatening to tear everything apart. And yet, the thought of giving herself to the river, of becoming something she couldn't even fathom, made her stomach churn.

The weight of the vial felt like an anchor, dragging her down. But the thought of losing everything—the village, her family, Kofi—kept her feet planted firmly on the ground. She couldn't run. She couldn't hide. Not this time.

Kofi's voice broke through her thoughts again, softer now, pleading. "Amara, please. I never wanted this for you. I should have stopped it. I should have warned you sooner, but I was too afraid. You're stronger than you think. You don't need to make this choice."

She closed her eyes, the words hitting her harder than she expected. His voice, full of regret, made her want to reach out to him, to forgive him. But there was something inside her, something colder and sharper, that told her she couldn't afford the luxury of forgiveness. Not now. Not when the fate of everything she loved hung in the balance.

"I *am* stronger than you think, Kofi," she whispered, the words laced with both defiance and sorrow. "But strength alone won't save me, will it? Not from this." She raised the vial, her fingers tightening around it. The liquid inside seemed to respond, swirling with an otherworldly glow, as though it were alive.

Kofi took a step back, his face pale. "You don't know what you're asking, Amara. Once you make the choice, there's no going back. You'll become the river's servant. Its vessel. The storm... it will be yours to control, but at what cost? You won't be the same person. You'll lose yourself."

"I already lost myself," Amara replied, her voice breaking. "When the river claimed me, when it made me its own... I lost myself the moment I stepped into its waters. The storm is already inside me. I can feel it, Kofi. I've been running from it, from the truth. But I can't run anymore."

Kofi's eyes softened, and for a moment, she saw a flicker of something—hope, maybe, or perhaps desperation. "There's another way," he said urgently, his voice trembling. "I can help you. Together, we can find another way to stop the storm. We don't have to make this choice."

Amara shook her head, the tears welling up in her eyes. "You don't understand. The storm is already here. It's not just the river. It's me, Kofi. It's always been me." Her fingers tightened around the vial, and she could feel the river's power responding to her, beckoning her with its insistent pull.

Kofi stepped forward again, his hand outstretched, as though trying to reach her, to stop her. "Please, Amara," he said, his voice raw with emotion. "You don't have to do this. We can still change everything. We can still fight."

But Amara didn't move. Her mind was made up. She could feel the river, ancient and unyielding, coursing through her veins, whispering promises of power and control. It was a seductive voice, and for the first time, she realized just how much she craved it.

The storm had come for her, and she had no choice but to embrace it.

With a final, resolute breath, Amara raised the vial to her lips, the liquid within glowing brightly now, filling the space with an almost unbearable heat. Kofi reached out, but it was too late. The moment the liquid touched her tongue, everything changed.

The power of the river surged through her like a tidal wave, consuming her from the inside out. Her vision blurred, her senses overloaded with sensations she couldn't comprehend—heat, cold, fire, ice. It was as though the very fabric of the world was unraveling around her, and she was at the center of it all.

She gasped, her body trembling as the force of the river's power coursed through her. The storm, the power, it was all inside her now. And as the world around her seemed to collapse into a swirling vortex, Amara understood the truth.

There was no going back.

The choice had been made. The storm was hers to control. But at what cost?

Kofi's voice, faint and distant, reached her as if from a far-off place. "Amara... no..."

But she couldn't hear him anymore. The storm had drowned out everything. The river had claimed her. And now, she was its vessel.

And the world would feel its wrath.

25

The Reckoning

The earth trembled beneath Amara's feet as the power of the river surged through her, twisting and shifting within her very bones. The garden, the trees, the very sky above her seemed to warp and buckle under the weight of what she had just done. She could hear the thunder in the distance, the storm gathering speed, its roar growing louder with every passing second. It was as if the very elements had bent to her will, but she didn't feel in control. She felt consumed.

Her breath was ragged, shallow, and her body trembled with an intensity she couldn't shake. The vial—the strange, shimmering liquid—had been the catalyst. The moment it touched her tongue, she felt the river invade every corner of her being. The power was unlike anything she had ever imagined. It wasn't just within her. It was her now, a part of her, melding with the darkness and light within. The storm was no longer a force outside her—it was alive in her veins, thrumming with a terrifying energy.

Amara staggered back, her vision spinning. The Winter Garden seemed to dissolve in a haze, its colors fading into darkness, swallowed by an overwhelming void. She raised her hands, feeling the tingling in her fingertips as the air around her crackled with raw energy.

And then, the world split open.

Lightning tore across the sky with a deafening crack, the storm above exploding into violent chaos. The wind howled, and the once peaceful garden was now a battleground of nature's fury. Trees bent at unnatural angles, their branches snapping in the gale force winds. The ground itself buckled, as though the very earth was shaking beneath the weight of the power she had unleashed.

Amara's heart pounded in her chest. She couldn't stop it. She didn't know how to control it. She had thought she could wield the storm, harness its fury—but now it felt like a wild beast, thrashing within her, refusing to be tamed.

Her legs gave way beneath her, and she fell to her knees, gasping for air. The power was suffocating. Every breath felt like fire, every pulse of her heart like a hammer striking steel. She closed her eyes, clutching her chest as if that might somehow anchor her in the storm's fury.

"Amara!"

The voice cut through the chaos, sharp and desperate. She opened her eyes, and there, standing at the edge of the garden, was Kofi. His face was pale, his eyes wide with fear as he looked at her. But even in the midst of the tempest, Amara could see the sorrow in his gaze.

"Kofi," she whispered, her voice hoarse and broken. She reached out a hand toward him, but it was useless. The storm had torn the ground between them apart, the very earth split as though it could no longer bear the weight of their connection.

He stepped forward, his movements hesitant, as if unsure whether the force that surrounded her would consume him as well. "Amara, please. This isn't you. You have to stop."

She shook her head, her body wracked with shudders. "I can't," she gasped, her voice raw. "It's too late. The river... it's too strong. I can't control it." Her eyes darted toward the sky as another bolt of lightning streaked across the horizon, illuminating the chaos around them. "The storm—it's inside me now. I can feel it, Kofi. It's like I'm drowning in it."

Kofi's eyes filled with anguish, but his voice was firm. "You're stronger than this, Amara. You've always been stronger. I know you can fight it. You have to fight it."

Her breath hitched. She could hear the pleading in his voice, feel the desperation in the air around them. But how could she fight something that was so deeply embedded in her? She had made the choice to embrace it, to take on the river's power, but now she realized the price was more than she could ever have imagined. It wasn't just a force of nature. It was a part of her, and with it, came a reckoning.

Amara closed her eyes, tears mixing with the rain on her face. Her entire body screamed, each breath a struggle, each heartbeat a battleground. *I'm lost,* she thought. *I'm no longer the person I was. I've become something else.*

The storm above her intensified, as if it sensed her surrender. The winds howled, the earth trembled, and the roar of the river filled her ears. It wasn't just the river that flowed in her veins anymore—it was the echoes of everyone who had come before her, the spirits of the land, of the river, of the forgotten ones. Their whispers filled her mind, urging her to give in, to embrace the destruction. They were a chorus of voices, speaking in tongues, their desires and their pain swirling in the tempest that was now part of her.

Amara's hands shook as she tried to stand, but the world around her was spinning, the power inside her too much to bear. Her head swam with visions—visions of the river's dark depths, of drowning in its currents, of the storm rising higher and higher, consuming everything in its path. She saw faces—her mother's, her father's, Kofi's—twisted with grief and fear. She saw the village, the place she had once loved, torn apart by the very power she had thought she could control.

"No," she gasped, her voice breaking through the chaos. "I don't want this. I didn't want this." She tried to push against the storm, against the force that gripped her, but it was useless. The storm responded to her, and in doing so, it tore at the fabric of her soul.

Kofi's voice was a faint whisper in the distance, drowned out by the wind. "Amara, listen to me. You have to let go."

Let go? She clenched her fists, the ground beneath her shaking. Her vision blurred as the power inside her surged, threatening to tear her apart. But then, something deep within her stirred—a flicker of the girl she had once been, the girl who had stood before the river and made her choice. It was a faint light, a memory, but it was enough.

"No," she whispered again, more firmly this time. "I *won't* let it take me."

With every ounce of strength she could muster, Amara focused inward, reaching for that spark of light, the part of her that was still human, still grounded. The storm roared louder, the river's power pressing against her with unbearable force. But Amara, trembling and exhausted, fought back. She reached for the light within, for the memory of who she was before all of this—the memory of love, of hope, of resilience.

And in that moment, as the world seemed to crack open around her, she felt the first stirring of control.

The storm didn't cease, but it faltered. The winds slowed, the lightning stilled, and the river's power—while still a part of her—no longer threatened to consume her. It was there, like a river flowing beneath her skin, but now she could feel it, *under* her control, not the other way around.

Kofi, his voice desperate and soft, stepped closer. "Amara... are you okay?"

Amara's breath came in shallow gasps, but for the first time in what felt like an eternity, she felt a flicker of peace within the storm. The chaos hadn't ended, but she had found her anchor. She could feel the power of the river, but it no longer defined her.

"I... I think so," she whispered, her voice hoarse but steady. She slowly rose to her feet, her legs weak beneath her, but she held her ground.

But even as she stood there, a part of her knew that this was just the beginning. The storm hadn't been stopped. The reckoning was far from over. She had gained control, but only for a moment. The river would still demand its toll.

And now, the true cost of her choice was beginning to unfold.

26

The Broken Heart

The storm had quieted, but the silence that followed was no relief. It was the kind of stillness that makes one aware of how much noise had been there before, how loud the chaos had been. Amara stood in the midst of the Winter Garden, her body still trembling from the aftershock of the storm that had almost consumed her, her chest heavy with the weight of the power she now carried. The garden around her had been torn apart—branches twisted, flowers uprooted, the once-pristine ground now scarred by the fury of the river.

Kofi was beside her, but she could barely hear his soft breaths above the ringing in her ears. His face was pale, his lips tight with concern, but there was something in his eyes—something darker. She could feel the distance between them, a space widening with every passing moment, a space that had begun to tear at the very fabric of their bond.

Her hands clenched into fists, the strange energy of the river still thrumming inside her, like an insistent heartbeat that refused to slow. Every breath felt like a struggle, each inhale dragging in the weight of what she had done, each exhale carrying with it a sense of growing dread.

"You did it," Kofi whispered, his voice trembling. "You stopped the storm."

Amara's gaze drifted to the sky, now only a faint, bruised shadow of its former self. The storm had not been vanquished—it had only been delayed, and it was still there, just beneath the surface, like a beast waiting to awaken. The river pulsed in her veins, its call a constant hum in her ears. She could feel it, deep within her, like an ever-present shadow. It was alive, and it was hers. But it wasn't just the river that haunted her. It was the cost of what she had done.

"I didn't stop it," she said quietly, her voice hollow. "I just... I just made it wait."

Kofi looked at her sharply, his eyes filled with confusion and something else—something close to fear. "What do you mean? Amara, you—"

"Don't," she cut him off, her voice suddenly sharp, almost pleading. She couldn't look at him, not right now. She couldn't bear to see the concern in his eyes, the way he was still holding on to the belief that she could somehow return to the person she once was. She wasn't that person anymore. She had crossed a line, one she could never uncross.

The wind picked up again, though it wasn't the violent gusts of the storm—it was a chill that seemed to slice through the air, as if the world was reacting to her inner turmoil. She wrapped her arms around herself, trying to hold the cold at bay, but it wasn't the wind that was freezing her. It was something else.

"You've changed," Kofi said softly, and his words struck her like a slap. "You're not the same person. I—I don't know if you even realize it yet, Amara. But the way you're talking... the way you're *feeling*... it's like you've... *given yourself* to it."

His words cut deeper than any storm could, but they were the truth. The river was inside her, and it was more than just power. It was a hunger, an insatiable need that had burrowed its way into her soul. She could feel it now, more than ever, like a dark thread running through the very fabric of who she was.

Amara bit her lip, her vision blurring with tears she refused to shed. She couldn't cry. She couldn't break down, not now. Not when the storm still hovered over them, waiting for its moment. She couldn't afford to let it take her—she had to keep control. But every time she tried to focus, every time she tried to ground herself, all she could hear was the river's voice, whispering to her, urging her to give in.

"You're right," she finally whispered, the words slipping out before she could stop them. "I've changed. But I didn't choose this. I didn't choose *any* of this. I didn't want to be the one to carry the river's power. I didn't want to be the one who had to face this storm."

Kofi's eyes softened, and he stepped closer, his hand reaching out as if he might touch her, might pull her back from whatever abyss she was spiraling into. But something in her recoiled at the thought. His touch used to comfort her, used to make her feel safe, but now, it felt like a reminder of everything she had lost, everything she was no longer capable of.

"You didn't have to choose," Kofi said gently, his voice breaking. "The river *chose* you. But that doesn't mean you have to let it define you. It doesn't mean you have to lose yourself."

The ache in her chest grew sharper, more insistent. It wasn't just the power of the river that haunted her—it was Kofi. She had felt it for so long, the pull between them, the bond that had once been so strong. But now, that bond was splintering, unraveling like thread coming apart at the seams. And she couldn't stop it.

"I don't know who I am anymore," she whispered, the words barely audible. "I don't know what's left of me. I feel like... like I've already lost myself to the river. There's nothing of me left to hold on to."

Kofi's hand hovered just above her arm, a tremor in his fingers as he fought to reach her. "Amara, don't say that. You're still here. *I'm* still here. We can fight this together."

But the truth was, they couldn't fight it together. Kofi didn't understand. He couldn't. He wasn't the one who had made the choice, who had embraced the darkness within her, the power that twisted her very soul. And that was what hurt the most—that she couldn't share this with him anymore, not in the way she had before. She was becoming something else, something he couldn't follow.

She took a deep, shaky breath, and when she looked up at him again, there was nothing but sorrow in her eyes. "I'm sorry, Kofi," she said, her voice barely a whisper. "But I'm not the person you knew anymore. I'm not... the person you loved."

His face twisted in confusion, disbelief clouding his features. "What are you saying?"

"I'm saying," she began, her voice breaking, "that I'm broken. I can feel it. I'm not whole anymore. Not like I was. And I don't want you to have to suffer with me. Not when I don't even know who I am anymore."

Kofi stepped back as if struck. His face drained of color, and for a moment, he said nothing. The storm in the distance seemed to pause, as if even the world itself was waiting for him to speak.

But when he finally did, his voice was tight, filled with the kind of pain she hadn't expected. "I never asked you to stay the same. I never asked you to be perfect. I just... I just wanted you. *All* of you. I never thought that when I said I loved you, I'd be asking you to give up everything for me."

"I haven't given up anything for you, Kofi," she replied quietly. "I gave up everything for the storm. And it's already taking me."

The space between them stretched, suffocating and cold. The storm, the power, the river—they all lived within her now. And it was too late to undo the damage.

The sound of Kofi's broken breath was the last thing she heard before the weight of her own broken heart settled in. The river was no longer the only force threatening to drown her.

27

The Unanswered Questions

Amara sat on the cold stone steps that led into the ruins of the temple, the weight of her heart heavier than any storm. The garden behind her was a tangle of broken branches, a graveyard of the beauty that once bloomed here. She could still hear the faint echoes of the river's call deep within her, reverberating against her ribcage, urging her to listen. But the world felt too silent now, as though the universe had forgotten to speak.

Her thoughts were clouded, disjointed—images of Kofi, of the storm, of the river's power all swirled in a haze. But through it all, one question lingered, more pressing than all the others. The question that had haunted her since she had first taken the vial. The question that had been on the tip of her tongue for days, but which she had never dared to ask.

Why?

Why had the river chosen her?

She could feel it inside her, like an unyielding current, always flowing, always pulling. She had thought she could control it, thought she could master it. But now, the river felt like something else entirely—an ancient being that had existed long before her, and would continue to exist long after her. It was a part of the world that had been lost, forgotten, buried beneath centuries of time. And yet, here she was, its unwilling vessel.

But why her? What had she done to deserve this? Was it fate? Or had she been a mere pawn in something much larger, something beyond her understanding?

A rustling sound broke through her thoughts. Amara didn't need to look up to know who it was. Kofi had found her again, and for a moment, she considered ignoring him, staying buried in her silence. But that wasn't who she was. She had never been able to ignore him—not when he looked at her with those eyes, filled with both hope and despair.

He approached her slowly, as though he feared that any sudden movement might shatter what was left of their fragile connection. His presence was a balm to her aching soul, yet it only reminded her of how much she had lost.

"Amara," Kofi said softly, his voice hesitant, "Are you... okay?"

The question was simple, almost too simple, but it held more weight than anything he could have said. She wasn't okay. She hadn't been okay for a long time now. And the truth was, she didn't know if she ever would be again. But she couldn't bring herself to say it out loud. Instead, she gave him a thin, forced smile.

"I'm fine," she lied, the words feeling foreign in her mouth. She felt nothing like fine. Her insides were a battlefield, waging war with the storm still raging inside her. "Just... thinking."

Kofi didn't believe her. She could see it in his eyes, the way he searched her face for answers. But he didn't ask. He never pushed her. And that, more than anything, made her heart ache. Because in that silence, she could feel the rift between them growing wider, deeper.

"Amara," he said again, his voice quieter this time, "I know you're struggling. I know you're scared. But you don't have to do this alone. We... we can figure this out together. We just need to understand why the river chose you. We need to understand what it wants."

The words hung in the air, heavy with the weight of their meaning. The question, the one that had been plaguing Amara since the beginning—*What did the river want?*

She turned her face to the sky, the gray clouds swirling above them, dark and oppressive. The storm that had begun in her was still there, a storm that was no longer just a force of nature but a part of her. It was not just the river that haunted her; it was her own fears, her own doubts, and the unknown future that stretched before her, like a cliff with no bottom.

"I don't know, Kofi," she whispered, the words barely audible. "I don't know what it wants. I don't even know why it chose me. I... I didn't ask for this." Her hands clenched tightly in her lap, as though the act of holding them still could stop the trembling within. "I thought... I thought maybe if I just embraced it, if I just accepted it, I could control it. But now I feel like I'm losing myself. Like it's taking more than just my power. It's taking *who I am*."

Kofi crouched beside her, his eyes filled with sorrow, but there was no judgment there—only compassion. "Amara, you're still you. You're still the person I care about. But you can't keep carrying all of this by yourself. You don't have to have all the answers. No one does. We just... we just have to figure it out together."

But the question still gnawed at her, deeper than the storm in her chest. *Why?* Why had the river chosen her, and not anyone else? Why had it decided to bind itself to her, to make her its vessel?

Her mind flickered back to the day she had first encountered the river, back to the whispers she had heard in the wind, the strange call that had seemed to echo from the depths of the earth. There had been a moment, a fleeting moment, when she had felt something—something ancient, something powerful—stirring beneath the surface.

And now, she realized, it wasn't just the river that had chosen her. It was something else, something older, more primal. *Something was watching her. Something was waiting for her.*

"I don't think we're just dealing with the river, Kofi," she said quietly, her voice tinged with fear. "I think there's something else. Something much bigger. Something... that's been waiting for me."

Kofi's brow furrowed, but he didn't pull away. He listened, as he always did, and that was what made it all the more difficult. Because Amara wasn't sure if she was ready to tell him everything. The shadows that had begun to move inside her were not just the river's—they were hers, too. She didn't know if she could trust herself anymore, let alone him.

But Kofi wasn't the only one who was searching for answers. The truth was, Amara herself was terrified. Terrified of what she had become. Terrified of what was yet to come. And most of all, terrified of the unanswered questions that loomed over her like a storm cloud, ready to burst.

"I need to find out," she whispered, more to herself than to Kofi. "I need to understand why it chose me, and what it wants from me. We can't keep running from this. We need to face it, Kofi. We need to know the truth."

Kofi reached out, his fingers brushing against her arm in an attempt to offer comfort. But the touch only reminded her of the distance between them, the space that had widened the moment she had embraced the river's power. She was no longer the girl he had once known. She was something else—something fractured.

"I'll help you," he said softly. "Whatever it takes, we'll find the answers. We'll face whatever's waiting for us."

Amara nodded, but it felt like a hollow gesture. She didn't know if she could find the answers—or if the answers would destroy her. But there was no turning back now. The questions were there, deep in her soul, and they had to be answered, no matter what the cost.

And as she looked at Kofi, she realized one painful truth. She might never have the answers. She might never understand why the river had chosen her. But in the end, it might not matter. The storm had already begun to rage, and its reckoning was coming for them both.

28

The Fading Light

The sky was beginning to darken as Amara stood at the edge of the Winter Garden, her body unmoving, her heart a tangled mess of unease. The air had taken on an oppressive stillness, the kind that makes even the bravest of hearts hesitate. The sun, once golden and warm, was now a faint, dying ember on the horizon, casting long, jagged shadows across the ruined temple.

The river, too, seemed to be holding its breath, its once-mighty current reduced to a quiet, brooding whisper. It was as if it, too, was waiting—waiting for something, or someone. The weight of the moment pressed down on Amara like a stone, and she felt the familiar pull of the water inside her, the eerie hum that never truly left. She could hear it now more clearly than ever before, its call growing louder, more insistent.

She had tried to ignore it, tried to push the unsettling presence of the river to the back of her mind, but it had become impossible. It was a part of her now, threaded through her veins, weaving itself into the very fabric of her being. She had thought she could control it, that she could hold the river back long enough to make sense of it. But the longer she waited, the more she realized that the storm inside her was not one she could simply weather. It was a force that demanded to be reckoned with.

Kofi's voice broke through the silence, soft and hesitant, as if unsure of how to approach her. He had been watching her for some time now, from the far side of the garden, but he hadn't come any closer. She could feel his gaze on her, steady and searching, but there was a distance between them that had grown too wide for either of them to cross.

"Amara," he called softly, his voice carrying across the stillness. "What's happening to you?"

She turned slowly, her gaze locking with his, and for a fleeting moment, she saw the flicker of concern in his eyes. His worry was palpable, his unease growing with every passing minute. But there was something else there too—something colder. Something that made her heart twist with regret.

"I don't know, Kofi," she answered, her voice barely a whisper. She couldn't look at him fully—not with the storm brewing inside her, not with the darkness threatening to consume her from within. "I don't know what's happening. All I know is that it's getting worse. The river... it's becoming part of me. And I can't stop it. I don't think I even want to stop it."

The words felt like a confession, as though admitting her loss of control was the only way to acknowledge the truth. She had given herself to the river, body and soul. And now, she was slipping into its current, unable to pull herself back.

Kofi's eyes darkened, his lips parting as if to speak, but no words came. The silence between them stretched out like a chasm, the weight of unspoken fears hanging in the air. He was searching for the right thing to say, but Amara knew there was nothing he could say to bridge the gap that had formed between them. The storm inside her was too powerful, too consuming. And it was only a matter of time before it shattered everything in its wake.

"I'm scared, Kofi," she said finally, the words slipping from her lips before she could stop them. She hadn't meant to say it, hadn't meant to let him see her vulnerability, but she couldn't help herself. The fear that had been gnawing at her for days suddenly surfaced, overwhelming her. "I don't know if I can control it anymore. The river is inside me, Kofi. It's taking over, and I don't know how to stop it."

Kofi stepped forward then, closing the distance between them, but still, there was a hesitance in his movements. As if he wasn't sure if he should touch her, if he should reach for her, as if somehow, by doing so, he might be pulled into the same darkness that threatened to swallow her.

"You don't have to face this alone," he said, his voice a soft plea. "We can find a way. We can find the answers. There has to be a way to stop it."

Amara shook her head slowly, the fear in her chest growing heavier with every word he spoke. "No, Kofi. You don't understand." She felt the river stir beneath her skin, like a restless creature that had been coiled tight within her, waiting for its moment to strike. "I *can't* stop it. It's too late for that. The river has chosen me. And I've... I've already let it in. There's nothing left of me. Nothing but the storm."

She felt a sharp pain in her chest then, a pressure that squeezed her heart until she thought it might burst. It was as though the very river that pulsed through her veins was trying to break free, to consume everything in its path. Her breath came in shallow gasps, each inhale feeling like it might be her last.

Kofi reached for her then, his hand finding hers, his fingers trembling as he grasped her tightly, as though he might be able to hold her together. But Amara could feel it—the distance between them was too great, and no matter how hard Kofi tried, no matter how much he cared for her, she was already slipping away. She was no longer the girl he had once known.

"Amara, please," he whispered, his voice ragged. "Don't do this. Don't let it take you."

She closed her eyes, a tear slipping down her cheek as she leaned into his touch, even as it burned with the truth she could no longer deny. The light that had once burned so brightly within her—her hope, her strength, her love—was fading, slipping away like the last remnants of sunlight in the dying hours of the day.

"I'm sorry," she whispered, her voice cracking with sorrow. "I'm so sorry."

For a moment, there was only the sound of their breathing, the soft rustle of the wind in the broken trees around them. And then, the faintest of tremors rippled through the earth beneath them, and Amara felt it—the river's call, deep and insistent, growing louder, closer. It was a siren's song, one that promised both power and destruction.

"No," Kofi said urgently, shaking her lightly, trying to pull her from the trance she had fallen into. "Amara, don't listen to it. You have to fight. You can't let it take you!"

But the pull of the river was too strong, too unrelenting. Amara could feel the darkness wrapping around her, like cold tendrils of ice, squeezing the last of the warmth from her soul. The light inside her—her connection to the world, to Kofi, to everything she had once been—was dimming. The storm was coming, and there was nothing she could do to stop it.

"I can't fight it anymore, Kofi," she whispered, her voice barely audible, swallowed by the wind. "It's already taking me."

The sky overhead grew darker still, the last vestiges of daylight snuffed out by the gathering clouds. The river's call reached its peak, drowning out all other sound, and in that moment, Amara felt the last of the light within her flicker and fade.

And in the fading light of the world around her, Amara realized the most terrifying truth of all.

The storm had already won.

And there was no escaping it now.

29

The Last Snowfall

The wind howled across the desolate landscape, a biting, relentless force that tore through the trees and swept the last remnants of autumn's warmth away. The snow had begun to fall again, this time heavier, as if nature itself was preparing for something far more terrible than the cold. Each flake was sharp, like fragments of forgotten dreams, scattering in the darkened sky. Amara stood in the middle of the garden, surrounded by the fragile whiteness that was quickly becoming a blanket of ice. The storm was far from over, and neither was she.

Her breath came in ragged bursts, visible in the frigid air as she watched the swirling snowflakes. She had been waiting for something—an answer, perhaps, or the calm after the storm—but nothing had come. There was only the gnawing emptiness that had settled deep in her chest, the gnawing feeling that something had changed, something essential.

The river's pull had not waned. If anything, it had grown stronger, more insistent. The power within her churned with a violent force, as though it were breaking free from every fiber of her being, tearing at the thin veil of control she still clung to. She could feel it, the weight of the river, and the pressure of the choice she had made. No matter how much she tried to fight it, no matter how much she wanted to reject its claim on her, she knew deep down that the river had won.

"Amara."

The voice, soft but persistent, cut through the silence like a distant whisper, barely audible above the wind. She didn't need to turn around to know who it was. Kofi had been following her for days, ever since the night of the storm when everything had changed. He had tried to reach her, to bring her back from the edge, but Amara wasn't sure if she could be saved anymore. She wasn't sure if anyone could save her.

"Amara," Kofi called again, his voice trembling with worry. "Please, we need to talk."

She turned slowly, her eyes meeting his. He stood a few paces away, his face pale, his expression torn between concern and something else—fear, perhaps, or disbelief. He had never seen her like this before.

"I know you're scared," Kofi said, taking a cautious step toward her, his hand outstretched. "But we have to face this together. You're not alone in this."

Amara shook her head slowly, the bitterness in her throat rising like a tide. She had heard those words so many times before—*you're not alone*—and yet, here she was, standing on the edge of something vast and terrifying, completely isolated. The river had taken hold of her in ways she couldn't explain, and now, as the snow fell around them, she knew that the bond she shared with Kofi could never be enough to undo the damage that had already been done.

"Don't you understand, Kofi?" she whispered, her voice raw. "It's too late. The river... it's inside me now. I can feel it, all of it—the anger, the sadness, the power. And it's not something I can control. It's something I have to become."

Kofi's hand dropped to his side as he took in her words. For a long moment, he said nothing, only watching her, his expression growing darker with understanding. Then, he spoke again, his voice thick with emotion.

"I don't care if it's inside you," he said firmly. "You're still *you*, Amara. The person I care about, the person I've always known. You can't let this thing, whatever it is, change who you are. You don't have to become it."

The wind whipped around them, sending a flurry of snowflakes scattering in all directions, and Amara felt a deep ache in her chest. It wasn't just the river she feared. It wasn't just the power or the storm that threatened to consume her. It was everything she had lost—the girl she had once been, the love she had once shared with Kofi, the connection to a world that now seemed so far out of reach.

"I wish I could be the person you remember, Kofi," she said quietly, her voice breaking. "But I'm not that girl anymore. I can't go back. Not now. I have to finish what's been started. I have to face this... even if it means losing myself."

Kofi's eyes flashed with pain, but his next words were steady, unwavering. "You won't lose yourself, Amara. I won't let you."

But as he spoke, Amara felt something stir deep within her—a dark, unfamiliar feeling, colder than the wind that bit at her skin. She glanced up at the sky, watching as the snow fell faster now, heavier, its purity turning into a storm of frozen despair. The storm was only a reflection of what was happening inside her.

"You can't stop it," she whispered, her voice barely audible over the wind. "No one can."

The air around them seemed to freeze, and for a moment, everything went still. The world around them fell silent, as if nature itself was holding its breath, waiting. Amara turned away from Kofi, her gaze fixed on the empty horizon. The river's call pulsed through her, louder now, thrumming against her very soul, its rhythm steady, insistent.

And then, with a sudden force, she felt it—the rush of the river inside her, rising like a flood, overwhelming her, claiming her. It wasn't just the river's power that surged through her veins, it was the knowledge, the certainty of the path she had to take.

She could feel the weight of the choice pressing down on her chest, suffocating her. It was no longer just the river that had claimed her; it was the path ahead, the choices yet to be made, the consequences she could no longer escape.

"You have to stop this," Kofi said, his voice desperate, his hands trembling as he reached for her again. "Amara, please. We can figure this out together. Just tell me what to do."

But she couldn't answer him. The words caught in her throat, and she could feel the last remnants of herself slipping away, lost beneath the cold weight of the river's pull. It was too late for explanations, too late for promises. The path before her had already been set, and there was no turning back now.

With a deep, ragged breath, Amara closed her eyes, letting the storm in her heart consume her. The last remnants of sunlight flickered out, swallowed by the clouds, and the snow began to fall harder, faster.

And in that moment, as the world around her seemed to collapse into the endless white of the snowstorm, Amara realized the painful truth.

This was the last snowfall.

The last moment of calm before the storm tore everything apart.

30

The Final Choice

The ground beneath Amara's feet had become a frozen wasteland, the once-beautiful Winter Garden now nothing more than a white expanse, shrouded in the cold embrace of the storm. The snow fell relentlessly, the flakes swirling around her like an army of ghosts. She stood in the midst of it, heart pounding, her breath shallow and ragged, as the river inside her pulsed violently. The silence was deafening, the world around her reduced to the sound of her heartbeat and the howl of the wind.

Kofi's voice broke through the storm, trembling, but unwavering. "Amara! Please, don't do this! You don't have to let it control you!"

She didn't turn to face him. She couldn't. The pull of the river inside her was too strong, its whispers too insistent. The storm that raged within her mirrored the one outside, and she knew—deep in her bones—that whatever came next, it would be the last choice she would ever make.

She could feel the power surging within her, an overwhelming tide that beckoned her to the water's edge. The river had been her tormentor and her salvation. It had become the blood in her veins, the breath in her lungs. She couldn't separate herself from it any longer. She had tried. She had fought against it, hoped for a way to break free, but now she understood. The river wasn't something she could conquer or contain. It was a part of her, and always had been. The path before her had been set the moment the water had first touched her skin.

"Amara," Kofi's voice broke through again, sharp with panic now. "I can't lose you."

The words hit her like a blow, but they were not enough to stir her. His voice had once been her anchor, the thing that kept her tethered to the world, to reality. But now, she couldn't bring herself to look at him. There was too much at stake, too much that had already been lost. The choices she had made had already set this in motion, and there was no turning back.

With a deep breath, Amara looked out at the snow-covered horizon. The world was so quiet now, as though everything were waiting for something to break, to shatter. Her hands trembled at her sides, and she could feel the weight of the decision pressing down on her chest. The river's call was deafening, its force undeniable, like a whisper that had turned into a scream. She could feel it rushing through her, pulling at her very soul, urging her toward the water, toward the final choice that loomed before her.

Kofi stepped forward, his hands outstretched, his expression a mix of desperation and determination. "Amara," he pleaded, his voice breaking. "Please. If you give in to this, if you let the river take you, I'll never forgive myself. Don't let it win."

For the first time, Amara turned to face him. Her gaze locked with his, and for a moment, everything else in the world ceased to exist. The storm, the river, the snow—it all faded into the background, and there was only Kofi, standing there with his heart on his sleeve, desperate to save her.

But she could see it now—the distance between them, the gulf that had opened up between them ever since she had first felt the river's call. He didn't understand. He couldn't. The choice before her wasn't just about her or him, it wasn't about love or loss. It was about survival. About finding the strength to face what she had become, what the river had made her.

"I wish I could choose you, Kofi," Amara said softly, her voice barely audible over the howling wind. "But I don't think I can anymore. I don't think I'm the same person I was when I met you. The river has taken everything, Kofi. And it will keep taking until there's nothing left of me. Nothing left of who I used to be."

Kofi took another step forward, his eyes fierce with pain. "That's not true," he said, his voice trembling. "You're still the same Amara. I know you are. I know you can fight this."

But Amara shook her head slowly, the ache in her chest growing with every word he spoke. "I can't fight it anymore. I've tried. I've tried to fight it, but it's stronger than I am. It's always been stronger than me."

The snow swirled around them, and the world seemed to blur, as though everything was slipping away, fading into nothingness. Amara felt the power of the river surging through her once again, a flood of cold and darkness that threatened to drown her. It was too much to bear, too overwhelming.

"I can't do this alone," she whispered, her voice breaking, the weight of the truth settling over her. "But I also can't keep running from it. The river wants me, Kofi. It's always wanted me."

There was a long silence as Kofi's face twisted in anguish, his eyes searching hers as if willing her to see the truth he was trying to offer. His voice, when he spoke again, was raw, filled with desperation. "Then let me help you fight it. You don't have to do this alone. Whatever it is, we can face it together. I won't let you go."

Amara took a step back, feeling the snow beneath her feet shift, the cold biting into her skin. The storm inside her roared louder, drowning out his words. She could see the sincerity in his eyes, the love and fear that mirrored her own. But love was not enough. It had never been enough. She had made her choice long ago, the choice to accept the river as part of her, and now, there was no going back.

The river called to her again, its pull undeniable. The storm inside her raged, a thunderous wave of power that threatened to overtake everything. She closed her eyes for a moment, allowing herself to feel the full weight of it. The power, the rage, the sorrow—the weight of all that she had lost, all that she had become.

Finally, she opened her eyes, and met Kofi's gaze one last time.

"I'm sorry," she whispered, her voice barely a breath. "I have to go."

And with those words, she turned, stepping forward into the heart of the storm. The wind howled around her, but she didn't stop. She couldn't stop. The river was waiting for her, calling her home. And this time, she would not fight it.

Behind her, Kofi stood frozen, his face a mask of heartbreak and disbelief. But Amara didn't look back. She couldn't. The storm, the river, her fate—it was all tied together now, and the choice had been made.

There was no turning back.

The final choice had been made.

31

The Winter of Forever

The wind screamed through the trees, a bitter, howling force that threatened to tear everything apart. The sky, once a delicate canvas of soft grays and blues, had turned an oppressive shade of black, as if the heavens themselves had swallowed all light. Snow, thick and relentless, began to fall once again, covering the world in a cold, lifeless blanket. Amara stood at the edge of the garden, her eyes fixed on the dark horizon, her heart heavy with a weight she could no longer carry.

The storm had not abated. It had only grown worse, its fury matching the chaos inside her. She could feel the river still coursing through her, twisting around her heart, drowning her in its relentless force. She had chosen this path, the path that would take her deeper into the darkness, into the heart of the storm, but now she wasn't sure if she could go on.

Kofi's face, desperate and full of pain, haunted her mind. His words echoed in her ears, his pleas for her to come back, for her to choose him, to choose love. But she had already chosen. She had chosen the river, the power that coursed through her, the call that had been with her from the moment she had first felt its touch. There was no going back. No undoing the choices that had been made.

But as the wind howled and the snow fell harder, Amara couldn't shake the feeling that something was wrong. The river had always been a part of her, but now, it felt different—darker, colder, more invasive. She could feel it pulling at her, dragging her deeper into its depths, but at the same time, there was a sense of foreboding, a feeling that whatever had been set in motion could no longer be controlled.

Her breath caught in her throat as she glanced down at the ground. The snow, thick and cold, had begun to form into shapes, patterns she hadn't noticed before. The ground beneath her feet shifted, and with a sudden tremor, the earth seemed to sigh, as if waking from a long slumber. The river's pull intensified, its grip tightening around her chest, suffocating her. She staggered back, her heart racing, her vision blurring as the storm whipped around her.

She had known, deep down, that this would come. The river was not something that could be tamed, not something that could be controlled by mere will. It was a force, an ancient, untamable power that did not care about the small, fragile lives of humans. And now, it was claiming her, its cold fingers digging into her soul.

But as she stood there, frozen and unable to move, a strange calm washed over her. It was not peace, not in the way she had hoped for. It was something darker, something deeper—a knowing. The storm around her seemed to fade, the wind less sharp, the snow softer. She could feel the river now, its presence inside her, wrapping around her like a cloak of ice. But it was not the same river that had called to her before. This was something else. Something older, more ancient, more powerful.

And in that moment, she realized the terrible truth. The river had not just claimed her. It had been waiting for her, waiting for this moment, for the Winter of Forever.

Amara's breath hitched as she turned slowly, her eyes scanning the garden, the once-beautiful space now unrecognizable under the weight of the snow. It was as though the world had been frozen in time, locked in a never-ending winter. The trees, once full of life, now stood bare and twisted, their branches like skeletal hands reaching out to the sky. The flowers that had once bloomed brightly had withered, their petals covered by layers of snow, their life extinguished by the chill in the air.

And then she saw him.

Kofi stood at the edge of the garden, his silhouette barely visible against the backdrop of the storm. His clothes were torn, his face pale and drawn, his eyes wide with fear and confusion. He had followed her, of course. He had never been able to leave her behind, even when she had asked him to. Even when she had chosen the river, he had stayed, clinging to the hope that he could save her, that he could somehow bring her back from the brink.

But it was too late.

Amara's heart twisted painfully as she watched him, as she saw the agony on his face. He was so close, but still so far away. The distance between them had never been greater, and yet she could not move toward him. The river held her in place, its icy grip suffocating her, drowning her.

Kofi took a step forward, his hands outstretched, his voice barely audible over the storm. "Amara," he called, his voice breaking. "Please. You don't have to do this. Come back to me. Come back to us."

The words stung, as though they were meant to tear her apart, and for a moment, she felt something stir within her—something deep, something human. She wanted to go to him. She wanted to run to him and throw herself into his arms, to feel his warmth and his love once more. But the river... the river inside her... it would not let her.

"I'm sorry," she whispered, her voice shaking. "I can't. I'm not the same anymore."

The words were like a knife in her chest. She didn't want to say them, but they were the truth. She had already made her choice. The river had already claimed her, and there was no turning back.

Kofi stopped in his tracks, his face a mask of disbelief and sorrow. "No," he whispered, as though the word itself could undo the reality that was unfolding before him. "You're not lost, Amara. You're still here. You still have a choice."

But Amara knew, in the deepest part of her being, that there was no choice left. Not for her. Not anymore.

The wind howled louder, a mournful wail that seemed to come from the very heart of the storm. The snow swirled faster, blinding her, and for a moment, she could see nothing but the white, the endless white. The river had consumed her, and now it was taking her into its depths, into the Winter of Forever.

With a final, mournful glance at Kofi, Amara turned away, stepping into the storm. The snow swallowed her whole, and the last trace of warmth and light disappeared.

The Winter of Forever had come.

And it was never meant to end.

www.ingramcontent.com/pod-product-compliance
Lightning Source LLC
LaVergne TN
LVHW021825060526
838201LV00058B/3518